Beauty and the

VAMPIRE

BOOK 2

DEMELZA BROWN
& EM BROWN

Beauty and the

VAMPIRE

BOOK 2

Chapter One

In the best of dreams, Daliyah walked beneath the bearded fig trees of Barbados with her grandmother.

In the worst of dreams, she saw the horrors of slavery.

And in the strangest of dreams, a dark shadow overpowered her, and after a flash of pain in her neck, lust flooded her body. An ache, a craving, blossomed betwixt the legs.

Daliyah blinked, feeling the remains of desire still moist upon her thighs. Stirring, she felt the silken bed linen wrapping her, the softness of the down in the pillows surrounding her. Sunlight gleamed from behind the curtains. She was still at Castle Blackbourne, a trespasser in chambers intended for finer guests. Reaching a hand to her neck, she found the bite upon her flesh felt different. Had she been bitten a second time?

Sitting up, she had the strange sensation that she had been asleep for some time. She recalled opening her eyes and seeing Mr. Brooke. Despite the curtains being drawn, she could tell it had been day. And then, when she had woken again, she saw Mr. Brooke once more, starting a fire in the hearth. It had been night.

Night. That was when the shadow came. Only it was no mere shadow the second time. It was... Lord Blackbourne. He had entered her chambers and assaulted her. She remembered struggling against him, and, knowing him to be far stronger, pleading with him. And then *he*— not a spider or rodent—had bit her.

She remembered feeling him inside her, filling her. And she had raised her hips to him, wanting more.

Daliyah shook her head. That had to have been a dream. And yet, it had all felt so *real*. Did she lust after Lord Blackbourne and not know it?

It seemed improbable. The only man she felt partial toward was Mr. Brooke, who had also appeared in her dream. He was the source of her desire. Had she transferred it to Lord

Blackbourne?

But in the end, it was Mr. Brooke to whom she had surrendered her desires, Mr. Brooke upon whom she had spent. Warmth rushed to her cheeks. He, too, had felt too vivid to be a mere dream. But would he have wanted to bed her? He had Miss Emma, Miss Cameron's other maid, more than ready to lift her skirts beneath him.

Wanting to clear her head, she hopped out of bed and went to a basin of water, which she splashed upon her face. Once more, she fingered the bite marks upon her neck. Those were real. Had everything else been real as well?

She went to the window and drew aside the curtains. Clouds of white filled the sky with no sign of menacing storms in the distance. If Mr. Phillips, her mistress' driver, could be found, they could perhaps depart Castle Blackbourne today. Daliyah knew not that she wanted to endure another night here. Perhaps Mr. Phillips' disappearance owed itself somehow to this sinister castle.

Though she felt as if she had not her customary strength, Daliyah dressed herself. She wanted to know what parts of her dream might have been real, and staying in her chambers would likely reveal little.

But when she prepared to leave, she found the door locked.

She tried it again. Why was it locked?

She knocked on the door and called out, to no avail. Pressing her ear to the door, she heard nothing. No one was near. She called louder and knocked upon the door harder.

After several attempts, she decided to open the windows. They had not been opened in some time, and the effort tired her. She thought perhaps she had not fully recovered from her prior illness.

Once she had managed to pry open the window, she looked out. She was quite high in the castle, overlooking the courtyard, far from the servants' quarters and on the opposite side of the castle from Miss Cameron's chambers. She would have to be quite loud to be heard, and her shouting would likely not be much appreciated.

As she pondered what she should do, she heard footsteps. Thank heavens!

A key was inserted into the lock. Seconds later, the door opened and in walked Mr. Brooke, carrying a tray with tea. He looked surprised to find her out of bed and dressed.

"You are well already?" he asked.

She returned a quizzical look.

"It, er, seemed you might have taken ill again," he explained.

"I must have been," she said. Was her illness what had caused her dreams to feel so real? "How long was I ill?"

"You slept through the whole of yesterday." He continued to look upon her with some disbelief. "How do you fare?"

"A little weak, but I will carry out my duties."

With a frown, he closed the door behind him and set the tray upon a table in the sitting area. "You ought not tire yourself. You would fare better with more rest."

"I have spent far too many days in these chambers. My mistress is undoubtedly displeased. Have you found Mr. Phillips?"

Mr. Brooke shook his head and poured some tea. "Would you care for breakfast? I could bring you eggs, toast, and butter."

"Thank you, but I think I should see to Miss Cameron first."

"She has managed these several days with Miss Emma. You need not worry."

His forwardness surprised her. He could not know Miss Cameron as well as she.

"Emma will appreciate the assistance from

my return," Daliyah said.

He handed her the tea. "She is faring well. Pray, sit."

Daliyah could only imagine Emma being irate and resentful, but perhaps she only presented smiles and cheer for Mr. Brooke.

"Pray, sit and have your tea," he reiterated.

She did as he bid and sat at the table.

Seeing the window open, he went over. "You opened this?"

"Was I not to?"

He closed the window. "It were best not to let the elements in."

Quietly, she sipped her tea. There was a stiffness to his tone and demeanor that had not been present before. She fingered her neck once more.

"I've been bitten a second time," she told him.

"Are you quite certain you've been bitten, or could you have wounded yourself?"

In her sleep? She supposed it was not impossible. She wished she knew what manner of illness had overcome her. It came and went haphazardly.

"I wonder if a similar fate had befallen Mr. Phillips?" she pondered aloud.

Mr. Brooke straightened, his countenance

stern. "What do you mean?"

"I wonder if he had become ill as well. Whatever ailed me brought about the most disturbing dreams for me. They felt extraordinarily real, and rather frightening. Perhaps Mr. Phillips took these delusions as reality and fled into the night?"

Mr. Brooke looked down at his feet. "It were possible. What manner of dreams did you have?"

"I think it too terrible to speak of." Despite her words, she felt compelled to reveal more. What had happened only made sense in a dream, but she could not elude how real it had all felt. "I dreamt Lord Blackbourne came into my chambers at night," she said.

Mr. Brooke turned a shade paler. "That is quite the preposterous dream indeed."

His reaction disappointed her. Till now, his words had never disparaged. But she supposed it was preposterous in his mind. For what reason would his master have gone into a maid's chamber?

"Did your dream have other...aspects?"

She flushed. "None worth mentioning."

He kept his gaze lowered. "I will bring you some breakfast."

She was about to protest that she could find

her own in the kitchen, but he had turned and was out the door. She supposed the sustenance might improve her strength. Eggs and toast sounded lovely, but she suspected naught but beefsteak could truly satisfy her hunger.

She watched the door close behind Mr. Brooke and then heard the insertion of a key.

He had locked the door.

Chapter Two

After he had locked her door, Addison released the breath he had been holding. A part of him wanted to go down to his knees and beg her forgiveness. He lamented his weakness in succumbing to his baser instincts, and yet, congress with Miss Daliyah had elevated her desirability. He would have preferred to find her revolting, for if, or when, the opportunity arose once more, he knew not that he could summon the forbearance to resist.

As Montague had said, her cunnie was indeed sweet. The memory of how her body had embraced his shaft stirred warmth in his loins even now. Everything about her had been sweet. Her lips, plumper than Miss Emma's, had tasted sweet. Even her scent was sweet, the aroma of her unwashed body far more mild than that of any other woman he had ever lain with.

Miss Emma had approached him again last night, but after having partaken of Miss Daliyah, he had lost all interest in the other maid. After Miss Emma had persisted in flirting with him and appeared she would not leave him be, he had been brusque with her. As a result, she had not greeted him this morning with the friendliness of past days.

The knob rattled behind him. Miss Daliyah was attempting to open the door. He regretted having to lock her in the chambers, but Montague had told Miss Cameron yesterday that her maid had taken ill once again. He was also to advise her today that Miss Daliyah was in no condition to travel and that they had best proceed without her.

With a sigh, Addison took himself downstairs to the kitchen. He had told her he would bring her breakfast, but he was not eager to return. She would ask him why he had locked her door or request that he not lock it again. What could he say?

While he contemplated possible answers, his brother rang for him.

"She is awake and upon her feet," Addison

reported to Montague, who had decided to take coffee on the veranda, an addition the fourth Earl of Blackbourne had had built.

Since the curse, Montague fed only upon blood. He had made a show of eating and drinking before Miss Cameron, but he took no pleasure in common foods. Today, he had said he felt like having a cup of coffee.

"She is recovered already?" Montague asked.

"It would appear so, and she remembers you entering her chambers, though she may think it a dream still."

"And did she recollect *your* presence?"

Addison flushed. He was undecided if he should feel relieved or disappointed that she had no recollection of him. "She made no mention of it. Have you spoken to Miss Cameron yet?"

"I have invited her to take breakfast with me."

Montague took a sip of his coffee. Addison waited for his reaction.

"Still bland, alas," Montague said, "but given that I had no interest in even trying in years, I am encouraged. I remember how I once enjoyed these dark and bold brews. I take it Miss Daliyah is secure in her chambers?"

Addison raised a brow. Confident in his

performance, his brother rarely questioned him.

"Of course," he replied. "You thought I would be neglectful?"

"It would be simple enough to forget to lock her door, though I suppose you've as much an interest in keeping her as I."

Addison flushed deeper. "While her door is secure, there is the matter of the window. It overlooks the courtyard, and she has managed to open it. She will notice the carriage when it is pulled to the front."

"Then move her elsewhere, into the dungeon, perhaps."

Remembering how distressed she had been when Jeremy, Miss Cameron's footman, had closed the door on her when she was down there, Addison replied, "Absolutely not."

Montague narrowed his eyes. "And why not?"

"She found it a distressing place."

"She has been down there?"

"I believe she went looking for the wine cellar and happened upon the dungeon in error."

"You have placed many a victim in the dungeon before. Now you choose to entertain qualms?"

Addison folded his arms across his chest. "Given her superior abilities to whet your appetites, her health and well-being would seem to be worth preserving."

After a moment of thought, Montague nodded. "It is remarkable that such attributes should reside in a simple maid. But if you think the window a problem, what do you intend?"

Addison thought for a moment before answering, "The carriage will have to be pulled round to the side of the castle."

It would be harder to load Miss Cameron's numerous trunks and portmanteaus there, but he would rather suffer the inconvenience than distress Miss Daliyah.

Leaving Montague to his coffee, he went to see to the carriage and the driver he had engaged yesterday to take Miss Cameron and her servants, Emma and Jeremy, to London, where Miss Cameron's aunt awaited her. Miss Cameron had been delayed several days in her journey. Wolves in the forest outside the castle had attacked the horses, leaving one of them injured. They had managed to escape and came upon Blackbourne Castle, a most fortuitous happenstance for Montague, who had been suffering from his dual hungers for blood and flesh and despairing that a cure would ever be found for his curse.

The woman who had turned his brother from man to monster had left them only the following words:

> For your want of goodness and love
> In body and soul shall you starve,
> Forever suffer a thirst unquenched,
> And burn in a lust un-doused.
> Till you find a true beauty,
> Shall you from your curse be free.

Miss Cameron was easily one of the most beautiful women in all of England. She had to be the answer to their prayers. And so Montague had courted her with success, promising to see her in London as soon as he could.

"I should be glad to be on our way," Miss Emma declared to Jeremy with a sidelong glance at Addison as he prepared breakfast for Miss Cameron.

"Indeed," Jeremy agreed. To Addison, he said, "I must say I do not envy your living in this gloomy castle, far removed from anything of interest. I rather think this place haunted."

"It is most dull and dreary."

"Do you suppose it were ghosts who took Mr. Phillips? What say you, Brooke?"

Addison covered the plate of toast. "I've never seen a ghost in these parts."

"Still, for Mr. Phillips to up and disappear like he did, one can't help but wonder. The wolves we encountered in Blackbourne Forest seemed unearthly."

Miss Emma shivered.

"Do you suppose Mr. Phillips met his demise because of them?" Jeremy asked Addison.

"Pray, let us not talk of such things!" Miss Emma objected. "And where is Daliyah yet again? Does she expect that I shall do all the packing after I have already spent all of yesterday attending to Miss Cameron's portmanteau?"

"Miss Daliyah took ill again," Addison said.

Miss Emma snorted. "A likely story. 'Tis but a ruse. Her kind, they are given to laziness."

"That surprises me. When she was healthy, Miss Daliyah took on duties not her own, offering her assistance though it was not required of her."

Unlike the two of you, Addison silently added. And he truly believed that the helpful nature he witnessed in Miss Daliyah was no aberration. Perhaps it was out of necessity. As an indentured servant, she had not the luxury of walking away from her situation. She had to earn the good graces of others or suffer the consequences. It amazed him that Miss Emma could conclude Miss Daliyah to be indolent when all evidence pointed to the contrary.

Glad to remove himself from the company of Emma and Jeremy, Addison brought the breakfast to the veranda.

"What a lovely setting for breakfast," Miss Cameron said to Montague as he pulled a chair for her. "How thoughtful of you to suggest it."

"The weather looked promising," Montague replied before taking a seat himself.

She leaned toward him and smiled. "Now you only need a true chef to perfect the breakfast. I mean no offense to your man, Mr. Brooke, here."

"None taken, m'lady," Addison replied as he served them.

"But a chef can do wonders for your meals."

Montague only smiled, for the truth was quite far from her statement.

"Have you anyone you wish me to give your regards to when I reach London?" Miss Cameron asked.

"As I hope to join you not long from now, that won't be necessary," Montague replied. "If the team of horses and the driver we secured are capable, I think you should reach London by the evening after tomorrow."

"I cannot thank you enough for all that you have done. I am certain my father will be in your debt as well when he learns of it all. I shudder to think what would have happened had we not come across your castle and you'd so graciously taken us in. You have saved us all, my lord."

"Anyone would have done the same when confronted with your charms, Miss Cameron."

She gave a contented sigh and murmured, "You are too kind, my lord."

Addison stood by and watched Montague take his time cutting his egg into small pieces while Miss Cameron partook of her breakfast.

"While I am happy to report that all is in order with the driver and carriage," Montague began as he applied several coats of butter to his slice of toast, "I regretfully have to inform you that your maid, Miss Daliyah, took ill again."

"I thought her recovered?" Miss Cameron returned.

"I know not the nature of her ailment, and I will certainly send for a doctor—I regret not having done so sooner—but Mr. Brooke says she is bedridden with the fever and chills. Alas, she is in no condition to travel, but once she is improved, I will send her to London."

"I could not possibly trespass upon your hospitality further. You have already been far too kind to her. It quite distresses me that she has become such an imposition."

"Pray, let it not be so. It pleases me to be of service to you."

Lashes fluttering, she smiled. "But surely if she can lay in a bed, she can sit in a carriage?"

Addison knew the conditions of the road from Blackbourne Castle to be poor. The jostling and bumping would make a person of health nauseous.

"As we know not the cause of her illness, I would fear she might prove contagious," Montague answered. "It is why we have kept her in chambers far from the rest of us."

Miss Cameron had straightened at the word "contagious" and pressed no more on having Miss Daliyah accompany them.

"I can engage the services of another maid if you require a second one," Montague offered. "I feel responsible for your loss as Miss Daliyah became ill upon my premises."

"My lord, that is beyond benevolent! I could not accept. It might be her own fault that she fell ill. You should not have to pay the price of her negligence."

Addison fisted a hand. As much as he deplored holding Miss Daliyah captive, a part of him was glad that she would be rid of Miss Cameron and the lot.

"I've another proposal, then," said Montague. "I'd like to purchase her covenant from you."

Chapter Three

Surprised by Montague's proposal, Addison felt his eyes widen. Neither Montague nor his father had ever employed an indentured servant before. His grandfather had at one time a young blackamoor for a stable boy, whom he had granted manumission when the boy grew older. It was not enough that they held Miss Daliyah captive, now Montague meant to own her as well?

Miss Cameron blinked several times and tilted her head before replying, "You wish to purchase my maid?"

"You could then employ a maid who can better serve you to your satisfaction," Montague replied.

"Daliyah is a trying maid, to be sure, but you

would not wish to have such an inept maid as she."

"I would think you have no interest in retaining a maid whose abilities you disregard so much."

"But I could not foist her upon you."

Addison would have thought her happy to have someone take Miss Daliyah off her hands and supposed it must be that she enjoyed berating the maid too much to let her go.

"Mr. Brooke has found her rather useful with chores about the castle, and I have been incredibly remiss in finding help for him. He has had to shoulder too much."

Here Montague looked to Addison, who wished with every fiber in his being that he could draw his brother aside to have a word with him.

"She has only a year remaining in her covenant," Miss Cameron informed.

"That is more than sufficient for the time being."

"What of her illness? Suppose it a serious one that could impair her, or worse?"

"I am willing to take the chance. While I've never had an indentured servant before, I see the merits of it now. Given our location, we have not always had the best fortune in retaining servants, who are easily frightened by our surroundings. There is more certainty with indentures. In that, you would be doing me a favor, Miss Cameron. I should be much indebted."

That appeared to appeal to Miss Cameron. She said, "And I should like nothing more than to assist you, but it was my father who had purchased Daliyah. I know not how much he paid for her covenant."

"I will pay him double, that he may recuperate his purchase price and more."

"Then I see no reason for him to object. I shall confirm it with my father, but let us say for the time being that she is yours. I hope that she will not prove a grave disappointment, but perhaps you will be better able to whip her into shape. I think I have been far too easy on her. Servants like her require a heavy hand."

Addison was glad when breakfast was over and Miss Cameron had left the table to change into her traveling attire. Montague pushed away his plate, which had retained all its contents save for a single bite each of egg and toast.

"You truly mean to purchase Miss Daliyah?" Addison asked as soon as Miss Cameron was gone.

"Why not?" Montague returned.

"Is it truly necessary?"

"You are much more at ease with kidnapping, then? By holding her hostage, that is what we are doing."

Having no response, Addison began clearing the table while he searched for one.

"And if she is my property," Montague continued as he rose to his feet and looked out over the veranda, "I've no need to return her to Miss Cameron. Ever."

"But we've no need to keep Miss Daliyah in perpetuity. Once we determine how Miss Cameron can break the curse, what do you intend with her?"

"She may prove of use still. But if I truly no longer require her, I can gift her to you."

Addison stiffened. "I could not in good conscience own another human being."

"That is because you have lived all your life as a servant and never owned anything of significance. And perhaps you have inherited too much of your mother's ingenuousness."

Addison acknowledged his mother, a gentle soul, had possessed almost a childlike innocence, always believing in the best of people and disinclined to see the ugliness in human nature, even when Montague's father had cast her aside.

Once done with clearing the breakfast table, Addison assisted with loading the carriage. When it came time to depart, Miss Emma said nothing to him and ignored the hand he offered to assist her into the vehicle.

Miss Cameron, standing before Montague, said, "I eagerly await your arrival in London, Lord Blackbourne."

He bowed over her outstretched hand before helping her into the carriage.

"If we find Mr. Phillips—and I have not given up hope that we will—I will, of course, send word immediately," Montague told her.

By the look on her face, Miss Cameron seemed to have forgotten all about her still missing driver. "I should be most grateful, my lord," she replied.

"*Bon voyage*," Montague said before closing the carriage door.

A minute later, the carriage pulled away. Miss Cameron waved her handkerchief at them through the window.

Montague breathed a sigh of relief when the carriage was no longer in sight.

"I can't say I shall miss her," he said.

While Addison shared his brother's sentiments regarding their former guests, he dreaded what he had to do next: face Miss Daliyah and inform her that she had a new master.

Chapter Four

It troubled Daliyah not that Mr. Brooke had yet to return with the breakfast he had said he would bring. She had never expected that he would serve someone in her station and appreciated his kindness. But she did fret that he was taking so long after locking her door. She found it odd that he had done so again, but what reason would he have for doing it on purpose?

She had heard some commotion outside and thought she had heard hoofbeats and the wheels of a carriage but could see nothing from her window. She paced the room with concern. Castle Blackbourne had unsettled her from the start, and her sentiment only deepened with the disappearance of Mr. Phillips. Something was amiss about the place.

Could Castle Blackbourne truly be haunted?

Her grandmother had talked of evil spirits from time to time, but Daliyah had never witnessed any evidence that such things existed. She believed man himself capable of enough evil.

Her thoughts turned immediately to Lord Montague. Like its castle, the master exuded an ominous disquiet.

Yet no one else, especially Miss Cameron, appeared troubled by the man.

"Thank heavens!" she nearly cried when she heard the unlocking of the door.

Mr. Brooke entered with a tray of coffee, toast, ham, and eggs. He closed the door behind him before setting the tray upon the table.

"Mr. Brooke," she greeted. "You must know that I am beyond grateful for the kindness you have shown me, but I am most eager to be of assistance to my mistress."

"Ah, on that note, I have good news, Miss Daliyah," he said with a broad smile that somehow did not reach his eyes.

"News?"

"You no longer have to serve Miss Cameron, whom I daresay seems like she could be quite the tyrant."

Taken aback by his unabashed—many would

deem impertinent—speech, Daliyah had no reply.

"You will find Lord Blackbourne a less demanding master," Mr. Brooke added as he set aside the items from the breakfast tray.

Daliyah started. "Your pardon?"

"He has graciously purchased your indenture from Miss Cameron."

She stared at the man. Did he jest?

"He feels responsible for your illness," Mr. Brooke continued, "and thought you should remain here till you are fully recovered, but then it occurred to him that Blackbourne is in need of additional servants, myself being insufficient—"

"No!" she cried when she realized Mr. Brooke spoke in earnest.

He appeared startled. "You are not pleased?"

"No!" she confirmed, panic quickly rising to her throat.

Her distress seemed to rattle him. "Your pardon. It did not appear to me that you enjoyed serving Miss Cameron. Frankly, I thought her treatment of you, and that of her other servants, to be more than unkind. You deserve better. I can promise to treat you with more civility than Emma or Jeremy have."

"It is not that. You have already shown

yourself to be a thousand times more agreeable. But I cannot work for Lord Blackbourne."

"I grant you he appears intimidating—"

"He could be the kindest of masters, but it cannot be!"

"It has been done."

Her eyes widened at the finality in his statement. "I must speak with Miss Cameron!"

"She has agreed to it and—"

Daliyah rushed to the door. Miss Cameron had been present when Mr. Cameron agreed that Daliyah could purchase the remainder of her indenture, but perhaps her mistress had forgotten?

Throwing open the door, Daliyah ran into something hard.

Lord Blackbourne.

For a second or two, she was caught in his arms, her gaze locked to his. The flare in his eyes made her catch her breath.

"Your lordship," she mumbled, stumbling back after he had released her. Dismay shivered up her spine. He was the last person she wished to see at the moment.

Blackbourne looked from her to Addison. "I take it you have informed her of her new circumstances?"

A muscle along Mr. Brooke's jaw tightened. "I have."

"Your pardon," she addressed Lord Blackbourne. "I must speak with Miss Cameron."

"Miss Cameron has departed."

She felt the blood drain from her head. Departed?

"She is en route to London," he informed.

"She— Mr. Phillips was found?" she asked, trying to wrap her mind about the new developments.

"I arranged for a driver and a new set of horses for her."

Daliyah grasped the back of a nearby chair for support. Miss Cameron was gone?

"But...she is my mistress," she said, feeling sick.

"She is your mistress no longer. I am now your master, and you a servant of Blackbourne."

"It was her father, not Miss Cameron, who purchased my covenant."

"She did not think her father would object, as I have offered twice what he had paid, though I will not have the benefit of the full tenure of your indenture."

"Lord Blackbourne, I beg of you, return me to

Miss Cameron!"

He frowned. "The matter is settled. I see that Mr. Brooke has brought you breakfast. I suggest you partake." Turning to Mr. Brooke, he said before leaving, "When you are done here, I expect you in my chambers."

After he had left, for several long seconds, Daliyah stood frozen where she was before crumbling to her knees.

"Miss Daliyah!" Mr. Brooke cried as he rushed to her side.

Despite an empty stomach, save for the bit of tea she had imbibed earlier, Daliyah felt like retching. Miss Cameron had abandoned her. Without word. Her only hope now was that Mr. Cameron would refuse Lord Blackbourne. Only then could she be reunited with the Camerons and have a chance to purchase her freedom.

But what if Mr. Cameron approved Blackbourne's offer?

She fisted her hand and brought it, trembling, to her mouth.

"Miss Daliyah, may I assist you to the bed?" Mr. Brooke asked.

She shook her head. She was not ill. She was dismayed.

"What may I do to ease your distress?" he

tried.

With her voice weakened by shock and dismay, she managed to reply, "You may return me to Miss Cameron."

Mr. Brooke seemed incredulous. "You desire her for your mistress?"

She turned to him. "My covenant. Miss Cameron's father had agreed that I could purchase the remainder of my indenture. I had but to earn another pound."

Her words seemed to wound Mr. Brooke. Looking away, he ran a hand through his hair and released a shaky breath.

"Come. Have some breakfast," he said after a moment of silence. Holding her, he lifted her to her feet and guided her to the table. She sat down upon the chair he pulled for her, but she had no appetite.

"Has Miss Cameron truly departed?" she asked him.

He nodded.

"I thought she was no longer in a rush. I thought she might want to wait to see what might have happened to Mr. Phillips."

Mr. Brooke's countenance darkened. "I think she no longer wanted to keep her aunt in London waiting."

"Yes, but she also seemed to enjoy your master's company."

"He has told her that he would journey to London. There, he expects to meet her father."

Then that was why Miss Cameron had been so willing to leave Blackbourne.

"If only I had not fallen ill," Daliyah thought aloud. "She must have been exasperated at my unavailability or she might not have sold me to Lord Blackbourne."

Mr. Brooke shifted as if ill at ease. "Miss Daliyah, I will endeavor my very best to ensure your time here at Blackbourne is as comfortable as possible."

She would look upon him with gratitude but was too filled with misery at the moment.

"If you require anything, do not hesitate to ask it," he said as he placed the cup of coffee he had poured before her.

She could only stare at it.

Mr. Brooke opened his mouth, then decided against what he had intended to say. After a moment of silence, he said, "I will return to collect the tray and dishes. Pray, you will feel better after you have had something to eat."

He took his leave. This time, he did not lock the door behind him.

Chapter Five

Montague looked out the window of his chambers with satisfaction. It was a gray and cloudy day, his preferred weather since the curse. A good day for a ride. And this time, he would not be accompanied by Miss Cameron's inane chatter.

"You could not have shown Miss Daliyah more compassion?" Addison demanded upon his arrival.

"I think I have shown tremendous compassion in allowing her to live," Montague replied, rather irked by his brother's tone.

"She is far more valuable to you alive than dead."

"Why should it matter to her who her master or mistress be?"

"She sacrificed—though not by choice—her freedom to serve you."

Montague released a long breath. What the devil was his brother talking of?

"She was to purchase the remaining year of her indenture from Mr. Cameron," Addison continued.

Was that why the maid had seemed so distraught at having a new master? "Miss Cameron made no mention of this," Montague said.

Addison snorted. "Why should she?"

Montague would not have been surprised if Miss Cameron, had she knowledge that such an arrangement existed for Miss Daliyah, didn't care in the least about her maid.

"It were plain that she would do much to please you," Addison added.

"Yes. Well, it matters not what motives or understanding Miss Cameron had on the matter. Miss Daliyah is mine now."

Addison pressed his lips into a dissatisfied line.

"You want I should return Miss Daliyah?" Montague challenged. "I have grown accustomed to hunting and feeding upon the villagers. Can you claim the same?"

Montague knew the answer before he had even posed the question. His brother was not at ease with the deaths required to keep Montague alive. He likely never would be.

As to returning Miss Daliyah, that was out of the question. No matter how unhappy it made Addison.

Relenting, he asked, "You will treat her with kindness?"

"Have I ever mistreated a servant of mine?"

Addison crossed his arms. "You have not always acted with kindness."

"I have only scolded where it was merited. I may have demanded superior performance from my servants, but I assure you there are other masters far harsher than I."

Addison became grim. "You fed upon Mr. Stonewall, a father to five children."

"You think I knew how many brats he had? Or that I willingly made them orphans?" Montague responded with anger. "If you had my curse, you would know how impossible it were to desist."

Addison lowered his gaze. "Forgive me. I know that you would not have harmed any of the victims if not for the curse."

Mollified, Montague said, "I can assure you

that I will treat Miss Daliyah as well as I can—better than Miss Cameron, certainly. Miss Daliyah will want for nothing. If you wish, you can take her into town. Purchase whatever she wants."

"What she wants is the end of her indenture."

Montague tried not to let his ire rise.

Eager to end their discussion, he said, "I mean to change into my riding clothes. Have my horse saddled. And if you wish to take the day to comfort Miss Daliyah, you have my permission."

At that, Addison promptly assisted Montague with his attire, no doubt eager to return to Miss Daliyah.

"If you were to become cured and no longer needed Miss Daliyah, there would be no need to continue with her indenture here?" Addison asked.

"You wish me to grant Daliyah her freedom?"

"Aye."

"If you like her, why not keep her?"

"She would be miserable."

As Addison retrieved the riding garments, Montague studied his brother. To put her happiness above his own, Addison's interest in the maid extended beyond a simple tumble. Montague considered if he had ever, or could ever, feel that way towards a woman. He would have doubted it...except he *had* felt oddly uncomfortable when he saw the dismay in the maid's eyes and heard the desperation in her voice. It felt...not unlike a kick in the gut. A minor kick hardly worth troubling over.

"Well?" Addison prodded.

"If I no longer require her blood or Miss Cameron is able to undo the curse, and you've no wish to keep her or her services, I certainly care not whether she stays or goes."

He wondered if he should be concerned that Addison was developing such a fondness for the maid. There were others he could have chosen to take an interest in—others far more beautiful than Miss Daliyah.

By the time he had finished changing his attire, Montague decided it would be more prudent to discourage Addison's attachment to Miss Daliyah. Addison had always possessed a more hopeful and optimistic disposition. For the time being, Montague chose not to voice his concerns. While Miss Daliyah was providing temporary relief to his appetites, there was no guarantee it would be thus on the morrow. What if the effects waned over time? What if his hunger managed to overcome him?

As the older, more reasoned brother, Montague would ensure that Addison did not raise his hopes too high where Miss Daliyah was concerned.

Chapter Six

Upon returning to Miss Daliyah's room, Addison found that she still had not touched the breakfast. Nor had she moved from where she sat. Her frown, downcast eyes, and slumped shoulders stabbed at his heart.

Taking the other chair, he sat down beside her and dared to take her hand in his. "As I've said, Miss Daliyah, I will do all that I can to see that you will not bemoan your time here at Blackbourne. His lordship was unaware of the agreement you had made with Miss Cameron's father. It is a devastating loss, to be sure, and Lord Blackbourne is not unwilling to consider a similar arrangement."

He wanted to be able to tell her that she

would have her freedom soon, but he did not want to give her false hope.

Miss Daliyah looked at him. "Truly?"

"I will press your case to him whenever I can."

She raised her brows. "His lordship will permit you to address him on such matters?"

"I have served him since I was a child. As he places a great deal of trust in me, I am in a superior position compared to most servants."

"Once again, I must thank you for your consideration, Mr. Brooke. There are not many in this world who would take pity upon or make such efforts for one such as me. Your kindness is beyond measure."

He would rather she not look at him with such awe and gratitude. He was no knight in shining armor. If she knew that instead of vanquishing the dragon, he assisted it, she would be horrified. She would look upon him as she would a monster.

The thought sickened him and he dropped her hand.

He rose. "Come, I shall brew you some fresh coffee as yours has turned cold."

She grabbed his hand to stop him. His pulse quickened.

"Pray, will you not partake of some of this breakfast?" she asked.

"I prepared it for you."

"It is too much, but I regret if it should go to waste."

He sat back down, not because he was hungry but to stay in her company. He accepted a slice of toast from her.

"When we are done, I shall move my articles back down to the servants' quarters," she said.

He almost replied it was not necessary, that she could keep her present chambers. He doubted Montague cared overly much where she slept. But Addison preferred her closer to his own quarters so that he could keep an eye upon her.

"What chores would you prefer to assign to me?" she asked.

How industrious she was. Her former confreres would have milked her situation to work as little as possible for as long as possible.

He almost jested to Miss Daliyah that she should not work too hard or Montague might wish to retain her services.

"You seem to enjoy being with the animals," he replied instead. "Perhaps you would like to walk the horses with me?"

Her countenance brightened. "Yes, please."

When in the stables, Addison told her, "Lord Blackbourne has taken his horse, but you ought never approach it, as it has a horrible temperament."

"Is it the dark brown horse?"

"Yes. That one has thrown Mont—Lord Blackbourne—several times."

Since the curse, however, the steed had become quite docile under Lord Blackbourne's command.

"The injured mare from the posting inn...when she is improved, we can return her to the inn," he said.

Miss Daliyah went to check on the mare, who had been injured in its attempt to escape the wolves while pulling Miss Cameron's carriage.

"She is much improved," she reported after removing the dressing from the horse's leg.

Addison went over to examine for himself and was surprised that the wound appeared nearly healed.

The mare barely limped when they walked her. Miss Daliyah appeared more at ease, though she spoke little. Suspecting she was still in shock over her new arrangement, Addison did not press for conversation.

After walking the horses, he went to feed the chickens while she attended to the cow. Though he liked her company, misgiving gripped his chest. She was too lovely a person to have to suffer her predicament. But what could he do to assist her?

Lost in thought, he had not noticed one of the chickens had escaped the coop.

"Damnation," he cursed as he went after the bird.

"Goodness!" Miss Daliyah gasped when he raced past her.

Together, they attempted to catch the surprisingly wily creature. The bird switched directions. In his haste to do the same, he bowled over Miss Daliyah, who had come up behind him. They landed upon the ground.

"Your pardon!" he said as he scrambled off of her.

Rising to his feet, he held out his hand to assist her. But he slipped yet again, pulling her down with him. She landed atop him.

A most marvelous position.

They were eye to eye, her breath over his. She had such bright, beautiful eyes. Wishing to remain as they were, he was still, savoring the feel of her body against his. She, too, made no move. A warm verve seemed to bind them.

"What is this about?"

At the sound of Montague's voice, they each scrambled to their feet.

"Damn fowl got loose," Addison explained, looking over to where the chicken, safely yards away, pecked at the ground in search of insects.

Despite the evidence of what he said, Montague looked skeptical.

"I have seen to my horse myself. Once you have recovered the bird, you may assist me in my chambers," Montague said before taking his leave.

"Have we upset him?" Miss Daliyah asked when he had left.

"He is often in a mood. Worry not of him."

Miss Daliyah went to the bag of chicken feed, scooped some in her hand, and approached the escaped chicken. She scattered it before the bird, distracting it enough for Addison to pounce.

"We make for a good partnership," he pronounced after replacing the bird in the coop.

She returned his smile.

"I hope you were not hurt when I knocked you over?" he inquired.

"I am unharmed."

"And when I, er, caused you to fall the second

time?"

She blushed. "Perhaps if I had landed upon the ground...but I did not."

Warmth churned in his groin. As they headed back to the castle, he marveled that he had the fortune of having her company. He had been so long without anyone save Montague, his appreciation of her was magnified. But even had he less loneliness, he was certain Miss Daliyah would still impress him.

But she might also be his undoing.

Chapter Seven

Walking past the door that led down to the dungeon, Daliyah shivered. Thinking the door led to the wine cellar, Jeremy had persuaded her to go in. She would not soon forget the terror that had seeped through her every bone as she beheld the skeletons—in tortured positions, it seemed—down there.

There were no dungeons in Barbados. None were required as plantation owners tortured their slaves in the open.

Stepping into her previous chambers in the servants' quarters, Daliyah unpinned her garments in preparation for bed and took stock of her situation.

Despite earlier sentiments to the contrary,

she was now glad to be returned to the servants' quarters and its inferior comforts. They were farther away from Lord Blackbourne, and if she had stayed in the chambers in the tower, she would have felt more beholden to his lordship. She wanted as little from the man as possible and was glad she had naught to do with him the majority of the day, which had started with a rude and devastating blow. Her freedom, within her grasp, had been set back a year.

But the day had ended on a brighter note thanks to the company of Mr. Brooke. They had returned the carriage horses to the posting inn, and Mr. Brooke seemed to have made every effort to make her smile or laugh. Making their way through Forest Blackbourne, however, made her remember their frightening encounter with the wolves. Mr. Brooke had assured her the wolves only came out at night. Nevertheless, she kept near him. He was strong and fit, and his smiles warmed her.

A pleasant excitement rose in her body when she recalled how his masculine weight had felt atop her, and then beneath her.

Nevertheless, her ultimate preference was to return to serving Miss Cameron. She hoped that Mr. Cameron would honor their agreement and persuade Lord Blackbourne to reverse his purchase. She would write a letter to Mr. Cameron, expressing her gratitude for the kindness he had shown her and her desire to finish her indenture with the Cameron family. Till then, she had little choice but to make the most of her current state of affairs.

Eager to begin writing the letter, she slipped a shawl over her shoulders and, taking her candle, went out to see if she could find paper and pen.

"Miss Daliyah."

She jumped, surprised by Mr. Brooke. His gaze swept over her briefly, taking in her thin shift. When he met her eyes, he flushed.

Clearing his throat, he asked, "May I be of assistance?"

"I wondered if there might be pen and paper about?" she responded.

"Pen and paper?"

"I thought to write a letter."

He raised his brows. "You know how to write?"

She nodded.

"You are a woman of surprising talents, Miss Daliyah," he remarked. "If you will follow me, I will find you paper, pen, and ink."

With their candles in hand, she went upstairs with Mr. Brooke. He led her into a library with shelves upon shelves of books, some needing a ladder to reach. Dark red drapes covered what seemed to be the tallest windows she had ever come across.

While Mr. Brooke went to a writing table, she set her candle down upon a table with several open books. She glanced down to see a drawing in one of the books depicting a woman being burned at the stake. Daliyah began to read:

Throughout time, men have toiled with the delusion that they can discover witches and take the necessary steps to destroy them. Witches, however, are not easily discovered as they have the outward appearance of humans. They exist alongside men, most of whom never have any knowledge that they have crossed paths with one.

To ensure the survival of their own kind, witches have sunk their claws into the world of men. They had adapted and blended into human society at all levels. Some have wed human husbands. Their descendants may or may not know that the blood of sorcery runs through their veins.

Next to the book that caught her eye was

another book on "The History of Witchcraft and its Consequences Upon Man."

"Lord Blackbourne takes an interest in witches?" she asked when Mr. Brooke approached her, holding paper, a quill, and inkwell.

Looking at the books, he frowned. "I think those books must have been carelessly left there by a previous servant. I should return them to their shelves, but here are paper and pen for you."

After handing her the articles, he swept up the books and strode over to a shelf near the window. She found it curious that he knew exactly where the books belonged. Perhaps he was the "previous servant" but was too embarrassed by his reading material.

"Do you believe in witches?" she asked when he was done putting the books away.

"Do I...witches?" he returned. He seemed uncomfortable.

To put him at ease, she said, "I do."

"You...?"

"Believe in witches. Not the sort that is often portrayed as evildoers wielding black sorcery."

"Then what manner of witch do you believe in?"

"I believe they are as capable of good as evil."

"Indeed?"

She was not ready to reveal that some considered her grandmother a witch. There were plenty of men who still believed that witches needed to be burned at the stake.

"Have we any evidence of their malicious deeds?" she replied.

Mr. Brooke colored. "I know not that they are capable of good, but they are certainly capable of evil."

The certainty in his tone surprised her. "You speak as if you have been witness to it."

He took her candle from the table, an indication that he was ready to leave. "I will say only that proof of their villainy exists," he said.

He took long, quick steps back to the servants' quarters. She wondered at how the subject of witches could vex him so? Had he been hurt by a woman suspected of witchcraft? They walked in silence till they were back downstairs.

"Forgive me," she said, regretfully, when they had reached their quarters. "I did not mean to distress you."

Standing outside his room, he held her gaze in his and appeared pained. "You have nothing to apologize for, Miss Daliyah."

"I thank you for the pen and paper."

He nodded and his expression softened. "This letter you wish to write, is it to a beau?"

She blushed. If he knew the dream she'd had of him…

"I've no beau," she replied.

"No? You must have an admirer—or several."

Her breath caught. He was staring at her more intently. The space between them seemed to have narrowed.

"If I do, they are not known to me," she said softly, her gaze dropping to his mouth. What would it feel like to be kissed by those lips?

His voice grew husky. "Miss Daliyah…I think you had best go to your room, for I am in danger of offending you."

Her pulse quickened. "Are you? In what manner?"

A tortured look crossed his face. She thought he might enter his room and slam the door behind him.

Instead, he placed the candles in one hand, cupped her chin with the other, and pressed his lips atop hers.

Warmth surged through her body. It had been years since she'd had a connection of consequence with another man. Though she would not have guessed it to be with someone like Mr. Brooke, she could not be more glad, for he was as kind as he was handsome.

He deepened his kiss. Heat pooled in her belly and below. With his lips, he parted hers, and they shared a breath. Then two...and three. It was more delicious than the sweetest custard, more thrilling than anything she had encountered since being in England.

But with a grunt, he tore himself away. "Forgive me. I should not have taken such liberties."

"There is naught to forgive," she assured.

He entered his room, set down his candle, and held hers out to her. He let out a breath and said, "I know you to be too kind to reproach me, but if you do not leave now, I will reproach myself."

She hesitated, then stepped into his room. It was the boldest action she had ever taken since becoming an indentured servant. She set the items she held upon the table. He stared at her, a mix of emotions swimming alongside blazing desire in his gentle eyes.

Looking up at him, she asked, "Will you not kiss me again?"

Dropping the candle, he took her into his

arms. His mouth descended upon hers with greater force. She clung readily, desperately, to his lips. He tasted and savored every inch of her mouth. With growing confidence, she returned his kiss. She could remain thusly for the rest of time, for the moment forgetting where she was, forgetting that she belonged to a man who sent chills down her spine, forgetting that her freedom had been snatched from her.

Mr. Brooke kissed his way along her jaw and down the side of her neck. She shivered, but not from cold. His hands were at her back, pressing her closer to him. She could feel the hardness at his crotch.

The wiser part of her advised against this. She had to work alongside this man. If they gave in to passion tonight, what consequences would follow? What if she lost his respect? What if he regretted laying with her? Awkwardness would replace the friendship they had formed. She had seen it happen to other maids who gave of themselves. One had even had her employment severed.

But Daliyah's dreams of late had inspired a flame within her, and her carnal inclinations would not be denied.

Sweeping her off her feet, Mr. Brooke carried

her to his bed and lay her upon it. Hovering over her, he continued to kiss her. She wrapped her arms about his neck and threaded her fingers through his hair while he reached a hand beneath her shift. He skimmed her lower leg before gently caressing her thigh.

She burned for him to reach higher. She strained toward him, letting her body speak her desires.

When his hand connected at last with her womanhood, she nearly cried out in bliss. She gasped as he fondled her there, savoring his every touch as he kissed the side of her neck. He lifted himself to look into her face while his patient stroking swelled the tension in her lower body. She could spend on his hand alone, but she craved a deeper connection. She reached for the buttons of his fall.

He brushed her hand away. It made her want him more. She tried again to undo his buttons.

"Miss Dal—"

Grabbing him by the head, she smothered his protest with a kiss. She pressed as much of her body to his as she could. He gave a relenting groan and made no further move to prevent her unbuttoning his fall, even assisting her in releasing his manhood.

Laying atop her, he positioned his shaft at her wet entry. To deter him from changing his mind, she kissed him more voraciously. In response, he pressed himself into her, just the tip at first, but she gloried in the penetration. He drew in a ragged breath before easing more of himself into her. She welcomed his hardness and felt herself growing wetter.

He plunged deeper and held himself there. Relishing the flexing and throbbing of his shaft, she embraced him with her cunnie, drawing from him a surrendering moan.

She sighed with satisfaction when his entire length was within her, filling her, stretching her, blunting her desire with his hardness. Gradually, he began to move his hips, building her arousal higher with each thrust and withdrawal. She found it easy to match his rhythm. Their bodies undulated and merged in a synchronized dance of desire. Her gasps quickened as the tension between her legs mounted.

Feeling her climax near, she ground her hips at him till the tension finally erupted, sending her into spasms of ecstasy. With a deep growl, he pumped himself harder and faster till he found his own sublime ending, spilling his liquid warmth into her as he shuddered and grunted. He kissed her brow, her nose, and her lips before collapsing beside her.

After the euphoria had settled, the doubts crept in, but she pushed them away when he wrapped an arm around her and pulled her close. She lay against him, glad to remain with him longer. In this manner, they fell asleep together.

She woke only once in the middle of the night. The candles had burnt out, and it was pitch dark. Nevertheless, she had the sensation that Lord Blackbourne stood near.

Chapter Eight

Riding his horse up to the stables, Montague found Miss Daliyah sweeping its entry. Hearing his arrival, she turned around and stiffened. She was not pleased to see him.

Nevertheless, she greeted him with a curtsy. "My lord."

He thought how easily he could take her now, here in the stables. He had ventured into her quarters last night, thinking to sample her blood and cunnie. But he had found her in the embrace of his brother. The scent of their congress still hung in the air, igniting his own desires further. He could have easily pulled her from Addison's arms—and wanted to—but decided not to disturb their slumber.

He dismounted and looked around to see that his brother was nowhere in sight.

"Mr. Brooke is tending the garden, but I can see to your horse," she said.

"You had best not," he responded. "Aries despises everyone, particularly strangers, and possesses a temperamental disposition. He twice injured my previous stable hand, and I suspect would gladly throw *me*, were he not fully aware that I am his master."

His warning should have caused her to step back. Instead, she moved toward the horse and looked upon the animal with curiosity. He gripped the reins tighter, should Aries decide to attack.

Instead of pawing the ground in agitation, as Montague expected the horse to upon Miss Daliyah's approach, Aries remained still. Perhaps the horse was tired, though Montague had ridden him far rougher before.

When Miss Daliyah reached out to the horse, Montague stepped between them. "I insist, Miss Daliyah."

At that, she relented.

"You may fetch water and oats for my horse," he said, "but do not go near him."

With a nod, she went to do as he bid while he led Aries into a stall and removed the saddle and bridle. He went to hang the items upon the wall. When he turned around, he saw that she had defied his orders, for she stood beside Aries, feeding him from her hand.

Too stunned to bark at her to keep her distance from the unpredictable animal lest she wanted her hand bitten off, he stood watching as Aries licked up the oats in the manner of a docile kitten rather than the raging equine Montague had always known.

How was Miss Daliyah able to accomplish this? Aries must not be himself.

"You say his name be Aries?" she asked.

Montague dared not move, lest doing so would provoke Aries into his customary disposition. The horse had seen many discouraged owners, initially taken by the majesty and power of the animal, only to readily have him taken off their hands.

"The Grecian god of war," Montague acknowledged.

"He is a beautiful creature," she remarked as she stroked the horse's mane.

Montague stared in disbelief. What had afflicted his horse?

"Miss Daliyah!"

They turned around to see Addison standing at the entry, a bouquet of flowers in one hand. Upon seeing that Miss Daliyah was feeding Aries, Addison appeared in equal shock. He looked to Montague in bewilderment.

"Aries is tired, I think," Montague said.

"Miss Daliyah has a way with animals," Addison replied with admiration in his tone.

Montague eyed the flowers. Seeing his gaze, Addison colored. "I was tending the gardens and thought Miss Daliyah might enjoy the blooms."

Montague noticed Miss Daliyah blushing. She glanced with concern at Montague, worried perhaps that he disapproved.

With a touch of irritation, Montague said to Addison, "I should like to change out of my riding clothes. Aries kicked up quite the dust and dirt in his gallop."

Addison nodded, then handed the bouquet to Miss Daliyah. Her blush had deepened. It became her.

Montague handed Addison his riding gloves, crop, and hat. When he and his brother were headed into the castle and far from Miss Daliyah, Montague turned to him. "Your partiality for her seems to have grown. I have never seen you pick flowers for a woman before."

"It benefits us to make her stay as pleasant as possible," Addison returned.

"She is not a guest but a *maid.* Given that I hold her covenant, she is, in effect, my property."

"She is one who calms your appetites unlike any before her."

"And what if that quality wanes? Then what am I to do with her?"

Addison was quiet.

Montague did not like to disappoint his brother. Of all the women, why did Addison have to fancy Miss Daliyah?

"You may lift her skirts all you like," Montague continued, "but it is foolhardy to form an attachment beyond the carnal." To cement his warning, Montague added, "I thought to feed upon her tonight."

"So soon?"

"Why not? She seems in good health."

"She has had a shock with regards to her new circumstances but yesterday. Why not allow her at least one more day of rest?"

Montague mumbled, "I will think on it."

They had reached his chambers. Addison put away the articles he held and assisted Montague with removing his boots.

"You have given her a proper share of responsibilities, I presume?" Montague asked from his chair.

"Aye. She accepted them all without complaint. I've not encountered a more hardworking servant. She enjoys tending to the horses the most, I think, thus I have relinquished all my stable duties to her."

Montague scratched his chin. "I wonder if a farrier could examine Aries and shed some light on why he is unusually subdued."

"Miss Daliyah has a calming effect upon horses. I've seen it with the injured mare that pulled Miss Cameron's carriage. The animal was agitated from its assault by the wolves and grew still with Miss Daliyah's touch."

With his boots off, Montague stood. "Do you mean to say she is capable of bewitching horses?"

Addison assisted Montague from his riding coat. "I think her capable of a special connection."

Montague snorted. "Such as the one she has impressed upon you?"

"You insist upon seeing her as nothing more than your next meal or tumble?"

"Why shouldn't I? What purpose would that

serve?"

Addison knit his brows. "I would still argue that treating her with kindness serves us better than not." He pulled from his coat pocket a letter. "I suspect she is not at ease with being here. She wrote this and asked me to send it for her."

"She can write?" Montague asked, taking the letter. It was addressed to Mr. Richard Cameron.

"She is no ordinary servant."

"That was apparent in the quality of her speech."

"She must have had a poor turn of fortune to have landed as an indentured servant. Someone thought highly enough of her to learn her such skills."

Breaking the seal of the letter, Montague read the contents, a plea to Mr. Cameron to overturn his daughter's decision to sell her covenant. She wrote of her devoted service to the Cameron family and, in a show of her desperation, offered to increase the compensation that had originally been agreed to for the purchase of her freedom. But she could offer no amount that could top his.

Walking to the fireplace, Montague tossed

the letter onto the logs to be burned when a fire was lit.

"You are correct," he said. "She is not partial to being here. But she has little choice—nay, she has *no* choice in the matter. Whether she likes it or not, Blackbourne is her new home and I her new master. You would do better to impress that upon her in lieu of spending your efforts gathering her flowers."

Chapter Nine

"Is all well?" Miss Daliyah asked when Addison came down to the kitchen where she sat peeling the potatoes for supper.

Realizing he must have looked disgruntled, he put on a smile. "I was merely preoccupied. I will take your letter into town tomorrow to be mailed."

She straightened in attention. "Thank you. Do you think I could accompany you? I noticed we could do with more sugar. If we had more flour, I could bake bread fresh here."

Baking was something Addison had never learned and had no interest in learning even had he an opportunity.

"That would be a treat indeed," he replied, but, thinking of the letter that Montague had thrown into the fireplace, he hesitated to agree to her request. "Alas, I have a great many errands to run."

"I should be happy to assist with any of them," she said with great earnest.

"Fear not, I do not expect that you will need to take on my chores during my absence."

She flushed. "It is not that, truly! I rather relish a change of scenery. With my having been ill here, it might do me good to take a walk about town."

He wanted very much to grant her what she desired. Perhaps he could have her shop in the market while he supposedly went to mail her letter.

She looked upon him with intense anticipation, almost as if she feared being left alone at Blackbourne with only Montague for company. A hazardous prospect indeed.

"Of course," he blurted. "I should be delighted to have your company."

She sighed in relief. "I know not what I would do without your kindness, Mr. Brooke."

She looked to where she had placed the flowers in a vase. "The columbines are especially lovely."

"Not as lovely as their recipient," he replied.

Her cheeks colored. She looked down. "I think his lordship does not approve."

Hang his lordship, Addison wanted to say.

"I think we have erred, you and I," she continued.

He quickly stood beside her. "If we have erred, the fault is mine, and I will bear the consequences."

"That is noble of you, but I think Lord Blackbourne must regret his purchase of my indenture."

"Do not mistake his moodiness for disapproval."

"Are you certain of this?"

"Quite certain. I have known him my whole life."

"And you think him as loyal to you as you are to him?"

"As loyal as a bro—master could be. You know him not as I do."

"Indeed, I know little of him save that my mistress is quite taken by him. To me, he...in truth, I find him rather imposing."

"Many do upon first meeting him. His finer qualities are not always on display, but they are there."

Looking deep into his eyes, she must have seen his sincerity. She nodded. "Even so, I think it wiser if we refrained from too much friendship."

Though disappointed, he understood her concerns. He rose and said, "If you wish, Miss Daliyah."

Having finished with the potatoes, she rose to her feet as well. "I could have the stew ready for his lordship in an hour. When does he prefer to have his supper served?"

"He may or may not wish to take supper. He feeds—er, eats when it suits his fancy."

"But it seems he has not eaten the whole day. He must be hungry now."

"He might have ridden into town and stopped at a coffeehouse."

She accepted his answer and only inquired once more after Montague when the stew was ready. When Addison confirmed his lordship would not take supper, Miss Daliyah ladled the stew for just her and Addison.

"Perhaps Lord Blackbourne has little affinity for my cooking?" she asked as the two sat down at the servants' table.

"I doubt it," Addison replied. "Your cooking is

far superior to mine."

She gave him a smile. "It seems I can always rely upon you for a kind word."

"It is merely the truth I speak."

She cocked her head to one side as she studied him. "Lord Blackbourne is fortunate to have retained a servant with such a congenial disposition."

"Now it is you who is full of kind words."

"Do you enjoy working for Lord Blackbourne, then?"

"I've never considered working anywhere else."

"Why not?"

He thought for a moment before replying, "I was born here, my mother having served the previous earl and countess. Blackbourne is all I have known."

"You've not had a desire to seek other opportunities?"

"In what? The army or navy? Nay, I am content to serve Lord Blackbourne. I belong here, with him."

"Your dedication is admirable. He must treat you well, then?"

"As good as any master, I warrant."

"I could not help but wonder as there are no

other servants..."

"Lord Blackbourne prefers quiet and solitude."

She nodded but seemed a little doubtful.

"He made an effort with Miss Cameron, though, to shed his taciturn preference," Addison added. "He can be moody. That was always his nature."

Her interest perked. "What was he like as a boy?"

"Clever, fit and strong in all sports and activities, gifted in so many ways. I fair worshiped him."

She smiled. It warmed his heart each time she did. He had never known a lovelier smile than hers.

"I wonder what the two of you were like back then?" she commented.

"I owe him my life. If not for him, I would be drowned in the pond behind Blackbourne Castle."

Her expression grew solemn. "Heavens."

"He took an interest in me then. I think, as he had no brothers or sisters, that he was rather lonely and adopted me for his brother."

"The two of you do have a resemblance, as if you were brothers by blood."

He started. "We do?"

She examined his physiognomy more closely. "The shape of your mouths and brows, as well as the structure of your cheeks. It is rather striking, come to think of it."

"We did spend a great deal of time together," he offered, though he knew that to be a farfetched explanation for their similarities. "He taught me how to hunt and how to ride. Many a time, he would sneak away from his tutors to take me fishing."

"How lovely of him."

Eager to have Miss Daliyah view his brother more favorably, he added, "Mont—er, Lord Blackbourne always passed his clothes to me. I sold them, of course, as it would not be appropriate for me to wear them about. And when the fifth earl no longer wished to retain my mother and me at Castle Blackbourne, Lord Blackbourne persuaded his father to keep us."

"I am glad to hear of his compassion. I think my initial judgment of his lordship to be less favorable than it ought to have been," she admitted. "I think it was because I found him aloof, but now I understand how one can be devoted to him."

He chatted amiably about his childhood

while they finished their supper, telling her the many games he and Montague would play, the best places to hide in the castle, and the stories Montague would read to him.

If not for their chores, he would gladly have sat several hours with Miss Daliyah, but he had to attend to Montague.

"Have you reconsidered feeding upon Miss Daliyah tonight?" he asked as soon as he stepped into his brother's chambers.

"I suppose I could wait till tomorrow," Montague replied. "I take it you wish to tumble her tonight?"

"I would, but she worries that you would disapprove if you knew."

"If Mrs. Connors were still the housekeeper, she would have turned the slut out. Though I had been above reproach in avoiding the temptations of asserting myself with any of the servants while at Blackbourne, it appears I am ultimately my father's son."

"I would you not judge Miss Daliyah. It was I who took advantage of her."

Montague raised a brow. "You forget I was there when you climbed between her legs the first time. I saw your hesitation, but she beckoned, and you came."

"She was under the influence of the poison your fangs injected into her."

"And she would not have lain with you otherwise? Did you ravish her against her will last night?"

Addison flushed. "A single moment of weakness should not condemn her."

"Why not?" Montague returned hotly. "It has for me."

They both grew silent. Addison did not like it when they quarreled.

"What is this?" Montague asked of the tray Addison had brought up.

"A stew Miss Daliyah made. You had not taken supper, and she thought you might be hungry."

Montague strode over and peered at the bowl. He stirred its contents and took a sniff. His curiosity surprised Addison, for food usually repulsed his brother.

"Dispose of the contents into the chamber pot if you wish her to think I have eaten," Montague instructed.

Addison did as his brother said. Later, he fibbed to Miss Daliyah, saying his lordship had enjoyed the stew.

As they stood in the corridor, each prepared

to retire into their rooms for the night, he asked her if there was anything she required.

"The castle can become quite cold at nights," he said. "Perhaps you require more linen to keep warm?"

She shook her head and gave him another smile. He wished he could collect her smiles in a jar to relish for more than the moment. She stood but an arm's length away, and he had to stop himself from reaching out for her.

"I pray you rest well, Mr. Brooke," she said.

"Addison," he replied. "As we will be working alongside one another for some time, we can dispense with the formalities."

She hesitated. "I think the formalities might prove helpful in our cause to keep our distance."

"You know not Lord Blackbourne like I do. He would not turn you out or sell your indenture to another merely because you and I have been familiar. He sees your work ethic."

"Does he?"

"I have, perhaps, extolled your virtues to aid his perception."

She seemed partially mollified. "Nevertheless, till I have earned his good graces, I think we should act with caution."

Addison looked down. Had she had a change

of heart toward him?

She placed a hand on his arm—a decidedly incautious gesture. "If the circumstances were not so tenuous, I would reconsider my stance. Without hesitation."

He quickly placed a hand over hers before she could pull away. They stared wordlessly at one another, their breaths uneven. He wondered, if he took her into his arms, if she would resist? But he wanted to honor her better wishes.

Reluctantly, he dropped his hand. She seemed equally reluctant to part.

"Good night, Mr. Brooke," she said.

"Good night, Miss Daliyah."

Once in his own quarters, he heaved a sigh. Perhaps his brother and Miss Daliyah were right, and it was wiser to cool his ardor. His feelings for her, not merely his desire to bed her, were growing with alarming speed. It had been so long since he had taken an interest in anyone, man or woman. For more than two years, he viewed others more as food for Montague than as humans. In the end, Miss Daliyah should be no different.

Montague did not warn him to cause him despair. As ever, Montague was trying to protect him from heartache.

Addison could only hope that it was not too late.

Chapter Ten

His brother's face fell when Montague told him the following morning that he would not allow Miss Daliyah to accompany him into the village.

The day was cloudy enough for Montague to enjoy his coffee outside on the veranda. Only, the coffee did not taste as good as last time. He wondered if feeding upon Miss Daliyah would rectify that.

"But she was looking forward to going," Addison said. "Will you not grant her this simple pleasure?"

"Her situation is already much improved from her previous indenture with Miss Cameron. I do not impose a great deal upon her or berate her as her former mistress did. She has her own quarters, the opportunity to lift her skirts to you. Is she not grateful for all this?"

"With Miss Cameron, she had the promise of *freedom*, an early end to her indenture. You read her letter. Did she not plead to be returned to the Camerons?"

"And what would freedom net her? She has nothing. She would have to seek employment. How would her life be any different with *freedom*?"

"I suppose…the liberty to go where she pleases."

"To do what? Find another employer who can treat her worse than Miss Cameron? Become a prostitute? As my servant, she has room and board. I would sooner have comfortable employment than freedom."

At that, Addison argued no more. Instead, he asked, "What will she do when I am gone?"

"There are chores aplenty. Now that we have an extra pair of hands, we can finally have the music room cleaned."

He had not entered that room in over a year. It once had been his favorite, for he enjoyed playing the pianoforte before the curse took away all of his interests. He owned one of the first instruments of its kind.

"And what will *you* be doing?" Addison added.

"Are you worried I will feed upon Miss Daliyah in your absence?"

"I would you wait till I returned. What if your appetites overwhelm you? If gone, I would not be there to stop you from going too far."

Montague doubted Addison could stop him, but he refrained from expressing this thought. "I was able to control myself last time, was I not?"

"But can we be assured you will have the same control?"

Montague stared at his brother, who had never questioned him this much before. "Are you worried what will become of your beloved bedfellow?"

Addison pressed his lips into a grim line before answering, "I worry what will become of *you* if you destroy the one person who has calmed your appetites."

"You need not worry. No harm will come to Miss Daliyah. But, regardless, it is my decision if and when I feed upon her."

At that pronouncement, Montague expected no further objection from Addison, who looked away in thought and seemed about to speak. Montague could feel himself becoming incensed with Addison's insubordination.

"You had best go," Montague said. "The sooner you return, the sooner you can rescue your precious damsel from my clutches."

With a frown, Addison turned on his heels and left. With equal vexation, Montague rose to his feet, nearly knocking over his coffee. It was damnably unfortunate and excessively inconvenient that Addison had taken a liking to Miss Daliyah. Montague could not remember the last time the two brothers had this amount of tension betwixt them. Addison fretted over the maid more than a governess would of her newest charge or a bitch over her newborn pup.

If he did not need Miss Daliyah, her blood and her body, he would gladly have given her to Addison. Surely his brother understood that? Addison had never before doubted his older brother's intentions toward him.

Montague thought of Miss Cameron. He had no desire to marry her, but if doing so could cure him, he would. Then Addison could have Miss Daliyah to do as he pleased. Montague would even approve marriage between the two if that is what Addison wanted.

For himself, Montague wanted proof that Miss Cameron was indeed his salvation before he made a commitment as grave as marriage.

Otherwise, it was much easier and far more pleasant to continue feeding upon Miss Daliyah.

Her blood was delicious and her body sumptuous. Heat swirled in his loins at the mere memory of how it felt to be inside her.

But, to make his brother happy, he would try his best to refrain till Addison had returned.

*****

Walking past the music room, Montague saw Miss Daliyah standing upon a chair, an armful of the drapes in one arm while she reached for the curtain rod above with her other hand. For a minute, he observed her backside and admired her figure. He wondered what she looked like without a shred of clothing?

As if sensing him, she whirled around, losing her balance in the process.

With quick steps, Montague went to catch her before she fell.

For several seconds, caught in the stare of her widened and ever-bright eyes, he could not move. Her mouth hung perilously close beneath his. Her cheeks reddened. With her feet still upon the chair and the drapes wrapped around her, she could not right herself without his aid.

She was helpless, and he could easily have kept her in his arms for as long as he wished.

Coming to, he set her back on the chair and tried to forget how her body had felt against his. He peeled the drapes from her and asked, "What is it you are attempting, Miss Daliyah?"

"I saw a tear in the drapes and thought to take them down for mending," she explained.

"Allow me."

He offered his hand to help her down. She hesitated, but it would have been rude of her to refuse, so she took his hand and stepped down. Once on the chair, he took down the drapes for her. It let in more light than he liked.

"Thank you, my lord," she said before heading away as if eager to leave his presence.

He stopped her. "Before you mend the drapes, I will have you dust the pianoforte so that I might play."

She nodded and, setting down the drapes, did as he bid. He watched her as she worked, taking in every inch of her, from the curls peeking from beneath her mobcap to the lovely cleavage above her décolletage. Though she had not Miss Cameron's beauty, he saw how Addison could be taken by her.

"Do you play?" he asked.

"I've not seen an instrument like this before," she replied.

"It's called a pianoforte. Do you play the harpsichord?"

She seemed surprised by his question.

"I thought whomever had you learn writing might have also provided you music lessons."

She shook her head.

"Where did you learn to write?"

"In Barbados. I was a servant in the manor house, and the master was a benevolent man."

She spoke with affection. He wondered if the man might have been her lover, for why else would a master of the house take such an interest in a servant?

"That is where you have learned proper speech," he remarked.

"Mr. Brooke speaks well too."

"When we were young, he spent a great deal of time in my company."

When she finished dusting the pianoforte, he bid her finish the rest of the room, then sat down at the pianoforte. The sheet music before him was Bach's "Sonata in D Minor." Setting his hands down on the first chord, he began to play.

Gradually, the memory of the piece returned to him, and he would occasionally glance from the sheet music to Miss Daliyah. He liked the harder passages, as it gave him a sense of accomplishment. Even while he focused on the notes, he felt Miss Daliyah's frequent gaze upon him.

When he finished, she applauded. "Splendid, my lord!"

Having played a few wrong notes, though only a practiced pianist would have noticed, he said, "Your compliments are unnecessary."

"Yes, my lord."

"I did not mean to chastise you," he apologized. "I made several mistakes, which I suppose is to be expected as it has been some time since last I played."

"Nevertheless, you played beautifully, my lord. It must have been a long time, as there was quite the amount of dust upon the instrument."

"Yes, well, I lost interest… Would you like me to play another?"

"Please, my lord."

He chose to play a sonata by the composer Mozart next. Miss Daliyah seemed even more delighted.

"You like the sonata in G major," he remarked when he was done. At her pause, he clarified, "The second piece."

"It was lovely," she answered.

Having finished dusting, she went to collect the drapes she had placed on the settee.

"Before you begin sewing," Montague said, "bring some tea up to my chambers."

"Yes, my lord."

He watched her depart and thought to play a brief prelude to give himself time to reconsider his directive to her. Instead, he rose to try to shake the warmth from his body.

He had wanted to wait till Addison returned, but she had ignited his desires when she fell into his arms.

It should not matter that Addison had not returned and was unlikely to for several hours. He had told his brother he could sufficiently control his appetites as to do no harm. He certainly had no intention of draining Miss Daliyah. He had to prove he could do this, or Addison would continue to question him.

Having reached this decision, he went upstairs to his chambers to await Miss Daliyah.

Chapter Eleven

Though occupying the same room with Lord Blackbourne had filled her with dread, Daliyah had suppressed her apprehension. She could not live all her days in fear of the man. Though he lacked warmth, he had been civil and did not constantly reproach her as Miss Cameron was wont to. Her perception of his lordship was colored by a dream she had had, but no matter its potency, it would not do to have reality distorted by fantasy.

She had been reminded of her dream and how real it had felt when she fell from the chair and into his arms. When she had looked into his eyes, she saw the same flare in his gaze as what she had beheld in her dreams. He looked...hungry. She had wanted to escape his arms but could not without falling farther from the chair.

She had received his command to dust the instrument with dismay and did her best to hide her disquiet while he spoke with her. She had no wish to displease him, to give him cause to change his treatment toward her or to sell her covenant to another. The further removed she was from Lord Blackbourne, the harder it would be to return to Mr. Cameron.

Her apprehension had dissipated, however, when he started to play the instrument, drawing from it the most magnificent of music, rich and full, thrilling in its variations and sweet with melodies. Lord Blackbourne only ever appeared somber to her, even in his courtship of Miss Cameron, but in his music, she heard parts of him unseen.

Earlier, she had been gravely disappointed when Mr. Brooke had informed her that she would not be accompanying him into the village.

"Will you be gone long?" she had asked him, dreading the hours she was to spend alone in the castle with Lord Blackbourne.

He must have sensed her concern, and seemed even to share in it. "I will be as quick as I can. I have to meet with Mr. Pierson, who oversees the collection of rents. Then I must pick up tools and horseshoes from the blacksmith. I shall make my way back after that."

"And my letter," she had reminded him.

"Of course. I will not forget."

She had watched him depart. True to his intentions of returning as soon as possible, Mr. Brooke had urged his horse into a gallop.

Although she had mourned losing her chance to go into the village with Mr. Brooke, she was glad to have had the chance to hear Lord Blackbourne play. The instrument had a lovely sound. While it resembled the harpsichord in outward appearance, the tone was distinctly different.

Daliyah placed a plate of biscuits and jam next to the tea on the tray, then carried it up to Lord Blackbourne's chambers.

"Enter," he said when she knocked.

The curtains were mostly drawn over the windows, leaving only slivers of light to penetrate the room.

Lord Blackbourne waved at a table upon which she could set the tea. After doing so, she turned to leave, but he spoke.

"Not yet, Miss Daliyah."

She turned back around to face him. Her pulse had quickened. The man who stood a few arms' lengths away was not the more subdued man at the pianoforte, lost in his music.

"I purchased your indenture from Miss Cameron, despite her evaluation of you as an inadequate maid, because Mr. Brooke spoke highly of your work ethos. How is it their views differ as to be near opposites?"

"I know not, my lord. I have endeavored to serve Miss Cameron to the best of my abilities."

"Do you mean to suggest that your former mistress is wrong in her assessment?"

Not wanting to speak ill of Miss Cameron, though she wanted to answer in the affirmative, Daliyah looked down to hide her true thoughts and replied, "I regret I have disappointed her."

His lordship eyed her more closely. "Then her recommendation should be deemed fair? Did you not steal petticoats?"

She looked up sharply. "There was a misunderstanding. Mr. Brooke gave me the petticoats."

"Mr. Brooke?"

"He saw that mine had soaked up the mud the day of our arrival. It had rained hard."

"My manservant is not in the habit of gifting petticoats."

"He said they were left by a previous maid

employed here."

Lord Blackbourne took several steps toward her. "Did your mistress lie, then, when she accused you of theft?"

"She misunderstood where the petticoats came from," Daliyah insisted.

"Did you explain their origins?"

"I did."

"Then she lied."

"She...chose not to believe me."

He now stood directly in front of her. She wished he would keep his distance. Why was he questioning her? If he had doubted whether or not she would be a good maid, why had he chosen to purchase her covenant?

"Would you say that Miss Cameron or Mr. Brooke has the correct assessment of you?" he asked.

"They have different expectations, measures of what they consider—"

"Choose one."

She hesitated. "I should like to think Mr. Brooke correct, my lord."

"And what is the source of his glowing recommendation?"

He drew even closer. Unnerved by his nearness, she stepped back.

"My lord?"

He followed. "Have you bewitched him somehow?"

Continuing to back away, she replied, "Bewitched? Do you jest, my lord?"

"Perhaps it would be more accurate to say that you seduced him."

She opened her mouth to speak but knew not how to protest. Her heart drummed in her ears. What did he know? What did he intend? He would not likely return a maid without virtue back to Miss Cameron.

Bumping into the wall behind her, she turned to her right, but Lord Blackbourne's arm blocked her.

"What manner of arts did you employ to secure Mr. Brooke's favor?" he demanded.

"None, my lord!"

His body pressed hers into the wall. She saw hunger clearly in his eyes. They were so dark, it seemed he had not pupils.

She tried to brush him aside to escape, but he wrapped his arm around her waist.

She could feel his breath as he said, "Come, my child, do you take me for a simpleton?"

His head lowered farther, as if he meant to kiss her.

"My lord, please," she gasped as she struggled in his hold.

His lips landed near her cheek.

"You would willingly lift your skirts to a fellow servant but not to the master of the house?" he growled.

She grabbed his arms and tried to push him away, but his strength was easily ten times hers.

"For your whorish behavior, Miss Cameron would have cast you out into the streets," he continued.

"I promise it shall not happen again, my lord!"

His gaze lingered upon her neck. "No, my dear. You need not worry of reprisals from me. I require only your dutiful submission."

She paused her struggles to contemplate what he had said. Was that the better option? Would she face worse consequences if she did not submit? Should she submit in the hopes that this would all be over sooner?

How naive she had been to think that indentured servants would fare significantly better than slaves! They were both at the mercy of those who held dominion over them. It was wrong, and she would be no willing party to it.

She kicked Lord Blackbourne in the shins.

He loosened his hold on her, more in surprise than pain, allowing her to wrest herself free. She ran for the door, but he caught her. The look in his eyes made her think he meant to eat her alive...

She watched in horror as two of his teeth extended into fangs. What was she witnessing?

He dragged her, pushing and kicking, toward the bed. She resisted, using the full weight of her body, but he tossed her, as if she were a rag doll, face first toward the bed.

Before she could recover from her surprise, her body bent over the edge of the bed, he was upon her, pinning her down. He brushed the tendrils of hair that had come loose from her cap, baring the nape of her neck as she struggled. Captured between his weight and the bed, she knew it unlikely that she could throw him off her, but she tried.

Until she felt ice piercing her neck. It turned into a searing heat as it spread through her body. She could not control her limbs, which twitched involuntarily. What was happening?

When the heat reached her loins, her struggles dissipated. Lord Blackbourne pulled her skirts to her waist. There was nothing she could do to stop him. Moreover, she did not want to. The hardness of desire pressed against her, *exciting* her. She lay still, confused, as he unbuttoned his fall. She had grown wet between the legs, the moisture allowing him to sink into her with relative ease.

She gasped at how lovely the fullness felt. She welcomed more of it, till he had buried himself to the hilt. She needed his throbbing member.

Slowly, he began a rhythm of withdrawing and thrusting, a motion that both grew and soothed her arousal. She pushed her hips back to grind more of herself against him. With each thrust, she climbed higher toward the peak of ecstasy. She reached it with a cry, her body devolving into violent shutters.

He must have reached his climax as well, for he groaned and trembled alongside her. But when she descended from her plateau of bliss, she found him still hard, and her own arousal not yet extinguished.

Chapter Twelve

Her body still warm with desire, she reached a hand beneath her hip for the bud of pleasure between her folds.

"My God!" he murmured when her cunnie flexed upon his shaft.

As if focused upon observing her caress herself, he remained still. The bud swelled with her attention. Tension knotted in her belly. He lifted her right leg onto the bed. It changed the sensation of his penetration. She moaned her approval. She could feel his body's craving and realized he had not yet spent. He resumed his thrusting. The room filled with their grunting, their panting, and the sound of flesh smacking against flesh. With her body, she urged him on till they both found their release.

He roared as he slammed into her harder, and she emitted her own cry as spasms overtook her from head to toe.

Closing her eyes, she made no effort to comprehend what had happened. She knew only that she felt satiated, pleased, and tired.

When she woke, she supposed that several hours had passed. She could see dusk fading into night through the windows. She stiffened. She lay in Lord Blackbourne's bed, her skirts in disarray. Moisture leaked from between her legs. She heard snoring.

Turning her head, she confirmed his lordship lay beside her. Gathering herself, she slid from the bed as quietly as she could so as not to wake him. Successfully, she made her way out his bedchamber and hurried down to her own quarters.

After wiping her thighs, feeling weak, she sat down upon her bed. Murmurs of desire still permeated her body. She touched the back of her neck and beheld drying blood upon her fingers. She had never been bitten by a spider or rodent. It had always been Lord Blackbourne with his...fangs.

Had the elongation of his teeth been real or an illusion? Even if the latter, she knew the rest had been real. He had ravished her, but not in a dream. And she had allowed it to happen—had *wanted* it to happen. Her head spun.

No. How could she have wanted it? She recalled struggling and trying to escape from his arms. Had he pierced her and infused her with some enchanted brew? She had never heard of such a thing happening to anyone, but there was much that she did not know of England, only that his kind was capable of the greatest of treacheries. What else might he do to her?

She ought not stay and find out.

Pushing herself to her feet, she grabbed her cape and hood and stuffed her coin purse into her pocket. In Barbados, runaway slaves, if captured, might rot in the cages for several days. If unlucky, their torture would be followed by death. Or perhaps the latter were the lucky ones.

What would happen to runaway servants? Would Lord Blackbourne send the dogs after her? She had to take the chance. For certain she faced an ominous future in Castle Blackbourne. She had sensed its malicious undercurrent from the beginning, and her instincts had been right all along.

As quickly as she could, she made her way into the kitchen, where she threw open the door to the outside. Rain clouds had darkened the sky. She knew not how much time remained before night completed its fall and the wolves came out. She did not hear them every night. If only she knew how to ride a horse! Then she could make her way through the forest faster. Should she wait till the morning? Could she make it through the forest in time when a part of her wanted to lay down and rest?

"Miss Daliyah..."

The words were faint and felt like a chilly whisper on the back of her neck. It might have been her imagination that spoke, but she decided not to find out. She ran out into the twilight and made her way to the forest.

At first, worried that Lord Blackbourne might have discovered her missing and decided to come after her, she avoided the path, but branches tore at her cape as if trying to stymie her. She undid the ties and removed her cape. In her haste, her body had warmed. She also tripped twice over brambles. Hearing a horse and seeing the light of a lantern coming from the direction of the village, she stumbled out onto the path.

"Miss Daliyah!" exclaimed Mr. Brooke. "What are you doing out here?"

"I mean to leave Castle Blackbourne," she replied, hoping that he would assist in her escape.

"Leave? Why?"

Knowing that Mr. Brooke revered his master, she hesitated.

His countenance grew ashen.

He knew.

Had Lord Blackbourne ravished other maids before her? Why did Mr. Brooke not warn her?

She took a step backwards, away from him.

He offered his hand. "Come, Miss Daliyah, we had best depart this forest before—"

The howl of a wolf interrupted him. Her heart sank. She had to choose between the wolves and Lord Blackbourne?

"Quick, Miss Daliyah! Place your foot upon mine and I will hoist you upon my horse."

Undecided, she could only stare at his hand. The wolves might be certain death, but returning to Castle Blackbourne meant...what?

"Miss Daliyah!" snapped Mr. Brooke.

She took his hand, and he pulled her onto the horse. With his arms around her, he snapped the reins. The horse broke into a gallop. Having never been upon a horse and sitting with her side to the saddle, she worried she would fall off.

She grabbed the saddle horn with one hand, though she knew it would hardly save her.

With a loud neigh, the horse came to a stop. Looking to see what had startled the animal, she saw a large wolf had landed in their path. Her mouth dropped at the frightening size of the creature. It snarled, revealing sharp white teeth.

Mr. Brooke dropped the reins and took up his musket. After quickly loading it with shot and gunpowder, he fired at the wolf, striking it in the shoulder. It whimpered and ran off.

Daliyah released a shaky breath, but her relief was short-lived. Looking into the trees and bushes, she saw several shadows.

Mr. Brooke worked fast to reload his firearm. He then fired it into the bushes, but not all the wolves were deterred. One of them leaped toward the horse, scaring the animal onto its hind legs. She was thrown to the ground, along with the lantern.

Mr. Brooke jumped off his horse to assist her to her feet, but another wolf had crept near. Not having enough time to reload, he swung the musket at the wolf, but yet another flew from the shadows, knocking him to the ground and catching his arm between its jaws. Mr. Brooke drove his fist into the wolf's face several times, but the animal hung on.

Seeing the musket on the ground, Daliyah grabbed it and struck the wolf upon its back. Still it did not relinquish Mr. Brooke, its strength reminding her of Lord Blackbourne. She tried to strike it again but was herself attacked. She landed on her back, a wolf atop her. It growled as it lowered its head.

She was certain it meant to take her face into its jaws—but it stopped momentarily, its nostrils flaring as it inhaled, taking in her scent.

With the musket still in her hand, she tried to whack the wolf on the side of its head. It jumped out of the way. Quickly, she rolled away and managed to scramble to her feet. She saw two wolves tearing at Mr. Brooke, his coat in tatters, blood everywhere.

For a second, she considered that she could try and flee herself, but she could not live with herself if she left Mr. Brooke to die.

She ran toward them but was again knocked down from behind. Her head hit a rock and all went black.

When she tried to open her eyes, she saw a shadow taller than the wolves. She heard one of them cry out after being flung against a tree. Her eyes would not stay open, however, and blackness covered her vision once more. She had the sensation of being carried, and no longer heard the growling and snorting of the wolves.

"Mr. Brooke…" she murmured before losing consciousness.

Chapter Thirteen

"**I** believe you a man of great courage, Lord Blackbourne," said the doctor, Mr. Thomson, an older gentleman with a receding hairline and spectacles that had slid toward the bottom of his nose.

Knowing Mr. Thomson would not venture into Forest Blackbourne at this hour, Montague had brought Addison to him. The doctor resided in a modest house and had a room he used to see patients.

"Thus, I will be only frank with you," Mr. Thomson continued. "Your manservant has sustained deep injuries of the flesh. While he can heal—even broken bones will heal in time— infection poses a severe risk. I have seen infection take down a man in two or three days."

Montague closed his eyes to hide his emotion. He would not give such a prospect consideration.

"As for your maid, the blow to her head is superficial," Mr. Thomson said. "She will have a good bruise but should otherwise be able to work."

Mr. Thomson looked over Montague. "And I can call for my assistant to bind your wounds, my lord, and give you a poultice for your cuts."

Montague looked down at the gash upon his arm. Intent on getting Addison to the doctor, he had paid no heed to the injuries he had sustained from the wolves. If only he had arrived sooner...

If only she had not fled.

He looked from the bed where Miss Daliyah lay comatose to the one where Addison lay a bloody pulp. Anger flared in his veins.

Turning to the doctor, he said, "You will be compensated for your care of my manservant, and a handsome reward awaits when he is mended."

Mr. Thomson adjusted his spectacles. "As I have said, his wounds are quite extensive, my lord. While I have no doubt a strapping young man such as he will heal from his bruises, infections can often prove deadly."

Montague felt his nostrils flare. "But surely you have medicines to ward off infections?"

"We have, and we will clean and dress his wounds often, but there are times when infection proves—" Mr. Thomson must have noticed Montague's glare, for he altered his tone. "I will endeavor to provide him the best of care, my lord."

"Spare nothing," Montague directed. "Mr. Brooke is the most devoted servant I have ever had. Treat him as if he were…my brother."

"Aye, my lord."

Montague looked over the doctor, hoping the man was up to the task. "I will take the maid back to Castle Blackbourne."

"Very good, my lord. Shall we now tend to your wounds?"

Montague looked down at his arm. A wolf had clamped its jaws upon him, shredding the sleeve and piercing into his flesh.

He shook his head. His wounds were nothing compared to what Addison suffered. "I can see to it myself."

"It would be no trouble, my lord. The wound upon your arm must be properly cared for, and you have quite the laceration upon your face."

"I would you address your efforts and attention to my manservant and not waste them on me."

Montague gazed upon Addison one last time, wishing with all his might that his brother could have the same strength and ability to heal that he had. But then his brother would also have his curse, and that he would never wish upon Addison.

Walking over to Miss Daliyah, he hoisted her over his shoulder and stepped outside to where Aries awaited him. He knew not what had happened to the gray his brother had ridden. The animal had either successfully fled or become a meal for the wolves.

After mounting his steed, he seated Miss Daliyah before him. She lay limp against him with her head on his chest. She had sustained scratches and bruises, somehow eluding the injuries the wolves had inflicted on others. Rushing into the forest, he had seen a wolf atop her, ready to tear her face off with its jaws.

Instead, the beast had paused. He recalled how Aries had reacted contrary to expectation with Miss Daliyah. The woman seemed to have a calming effect on animals.

On the ride back to the castle, she groaned a

few times and murmured the name of his brother. Montague pressed his lips together. If his brother did not lie a mangled mess with a fair chance of meeting Death, Montague might have been gratified of her concern for Addison.

But *she* was the reason his brother had been attacked by wolves. *She* was at fault. And she would pay the consequences.

Chapter Fourteen

As Daliyah fluttered her eyes open, she noticed first how her head ached. She heard the steady patter of rain outside. Next, she felt the cold. And her arms were sore. She sensed the glow of a candlelight amidst the dark.

Opening her eyes farther, she saw a man sitting in a simple wooden chair several feet from her, a candle beside him upon the floor, his arm bandaged.

Suddenly, she remembered the wolves. They had attacked her and Mr. Brooke. Had that been real?

"Mr. Brooke?" she voiced weakly.

"If only," returned the man sitting in the chair.

Her heart sank. It was Lord Blackbourne.

He was the one she had hoped to escape. She had even risked her life by venturing into Forest Blackbourne, where she had come upon Mr. Brooke. She last remembered him upon the ground struggling against two wolves. Dear God...

She dreaded the answer but had to ask, "What has happened to Mr. Brooke?"

"Does it worry you what happened to him?" his lordship inquired.

"Of course."

"Then you should have thought of him before you ran into the forest."

Anger flared in his eyes. She wanted to know what had happened to Mr. Brooke but almost dared not ask. Then she realized why her arms felt sore: they were shackled together at the wrists above her head. She stood in a cell with stone walls and no windows.

It could only be in...the dungeon.

No! She struggled to free herself from the shackles. "Please, my lord—"

He rose from the chair and ambled toward her. "You knew the forest to be infested with bloodthirsty wolves. You knew Mr. Brooke would do all that he could to protect you. You knew this because you seduced him into fancying you."

"I did not intend—"

"You did not willingly lift your skirts beneath him?"

How could she possibly provide a response that would satisfy him?

"Is he...?" she asked.

"At Death's doorstep? Quite possibly."

She gasped. Dismay flooded her. "Is he here? Perhaps I can—"

"He is in the care of a doctor at present. What need has he of a harlot?"

Lord Blackbourne stood mere inches from her. She saw slash marks upon the side of his face, no doubt the result of a wolf's claws.

"I knew not that I would come upon him," she said.

"Liar! No one in their right mind would venture into Forest Blackbourne."

"I speak true! I would never wish him harm. I feared—"

But he had grasped her by the throat, making speech difficult. She saw in horror as his teeth elongated into fangs. What manner of man—nay, monster—was he?

"Addison risked his life for you," Blackbourne

snarled as his face came ever closer to hers. "If he should perish, his death will be writ upon your conscience."

He pressed his body into hers and ground the hardness between his legs against her. Trapped between him and the wall, her body could not escape his, and any effort she made to wriggle from him only seemed to ignite the fire in his eyes more. His free hand dropped to the buttons of his fall.

"Lord Blackbourne, if I could—" she tried, till he tightened his grip upon her throat.

"Save your whorish breath for someone who cares to listen—'twould be Addison, but you have seen to his demise."

He pulled up her skirts. She felt his member against her belly.

"Your lordship—" Her wrists scraped against the shackles as she tried to squirm free and throw his body off of her. "Your lordship!"

Releasing her throat, he grabbed her thighs and hoisted them up so that he could spear into her. She cried out at the rough intrusion. Meeting his gaze, his countenance filled with rage, she implored him with her eyes. If there was an ounce of mercy in him, she begged to find it.

He faltered and seemed to be rendered immobile by an internal war. He blinked several times. A muscle along his jaw rippled. Then, lowering his head, he sank his fangs into her neck. Ice followed by heat filled her veins. Desire washed over her. This was the devil's work...

But her mind soon ceased to comprehend, ceased to care for thoughts. All she wanted was to feel his shaft deeper inside her. Her cunnie rippled along his length, a siren's invitation. Accepting it, he thrust farther into her warmth, which soon dripped with arousal. Holding her legs up, he shoved and ground her against the wall. She no longer writhed for escape but to impale herself harder upon him.

"My God," he grunted as they ground and bucked their way to release.

She spent first, trembling in euphoria as tension uncoiled from her head to her toes. With short, hard thrusts, he followed with his climax. He roared and ground himself deep into her, his liquid heat melding with hers. Bliss enveloped them as one, and she thought the beating of his heart to be her own. Her cunnie pulsed about his throbbing member as their panting converged, then diverged. He rested his perspiring brow to hers. A shudder went through him before he set her legs down.

After several minutes, when his shaft had softened, he seemed to emerge from his daze. He buttoned the fall of his breeches and looked upon her. The warmth of lust had faded, replaced with an icy anger. He turned and went to pick up the candle. She watched him head to the door.

He meant to leave her here?

"Lord Blackbourne, please!" she cried.

But he closed the door behind him, leaving her in blackness.

Chapter Fifteen

Montague sat in the darkness of his chambers, Miss Daliyah's pleas as he closed the cell door still echoing in his ears. Addison had said she'd had a fright when she had accidentally stumbled upon the dungeon. But a night in the dungeon could not compare to what Addison presently endured. Montague could have made it worse for her and placed her amidst the skeletons in the adjoining cell. But he had spared her the worst.

He had fully intended to show her no mercy, had planned to revel in her suffering and ravage her brutally by withholding the arousal he knew he could impose for her. Perhaps he preferred not to hear her pleas, but he could not wholly dismiss the stab of desperation he had felt—not his own, but *hers*.

Thus, he had changed his mind and bit her, flooding her with desire. He did not regret his change of heart, for his climax always felt more magnificent when she spent, but he had thought he would derive more pleasure from her pain.

Rising from his chair, Montague paced the room. He wondered how his brother fared. Was Mr. Thomson a good enough doctor?

Helplessness tore at him. He hated the feeling. If he should lose Addison...he would feel it more than the loss of his father, or even his mother before him. If only that foolish Miss Daliyah had not run off into the forest! If only his brother had heeded his advice and not taken a fancy to the maid. How much of Addison's efforts to save her was for her sake versus his?

Of course, Addison would do anything for his brother. His attachment to Miss Daliyah could not best years of brotherly love.

Nonetheless, Addison would be glad to know that Montague had resisted feeding upon Miss Daliyah. Indeed, that appetite had not reared its ugly head in the dungeon. Possibly because Montague had already partaken of her blood earlier.

Addison would be dismayed, however, to

learn that Miss Daliyah had been left in the dungeon.

She is not your concern, Montague wanted to remind Addison.

But after several minutes of pacing, Montague lit a lantern and headed down to the dungeon. He found Miss Daliyah shivering, her eyes shut tightly as if a horrific vision threatened her. Setting down the lantern, he went to unlock her shackles. She collapsed into his arms. He scooped her up, picked up the lantern, and returned upstairs.

He had the largest, most comfortable bed in the castle, so he decided to deposit her there. She continued to tremble as if cold. After pulling the bedclothes over her, he started a fire and took the warming pan hanging near the hearth. After filling it with embers, he placed it beneath the bedclothes. As the heat did not last, he had to empty and refill the warming pan several times.

Miss Daliyah finally stopped shivering and fell asleep. Montague spent the night on the settee, watching as she slept.

When she opened her eyes and saw him, fear immediately overcame her. She would, no doubt, never greet Addison with such an expression upon waking, Montague thought to himself wryly.

He had an odd impulse to address what had transpired last night but knew not what he would say. Instead, he said, "You will want breakfast, I gather."

She shook her head. He could see her desire to flee, but they both knew she had nowhere to go.

"Nevertheless, sustenance will do you good," he said. "Are you able to walk?"

"Aye, my lord."

Carefully, as if worried that a sudden movement would make him pounce upon her, she slid from the bed.

He rose to his feet but stayed his distance from her. "Come."

She followed him out of his chambers and down into the kitchen, keeping him in her gaze at all times.

Addison would probably be tripping over himself to make her breakfast, but Montague had never so much as boiled water himself.

"Make yourself some tea or coffee," he directed her.

Remembering her place, she asked, "What would your lordship prefer?"

"I require nothing. Do as you please."

"I will need to fetch water."

Considering that she might make an attempt to escape once outside, he said, "I will go with you."

She took a bucket, and they walked outside to the well. The rainclouds of last night had wrung themselves dry, but light gray clouds blocked the sun, keeping it from warming the air. He watched her lower the bucket, then tug upon the rope to pull up the filled vessel. To hasten the job, he took the rope from her and hauled the bucket of water up himself.

"Thank you, my lord," she murmured as she reached for the water.

"I will take it in," he told her.

She looked surprised. For good reason, he supposed. He could not remember the last time he had undertaken the task of a servant.

When she remained still, he headed inside so that she had no choice but to follow. Back in the kitchen, she poured water into a kettle and started a fire in the stove while he watched.

"What will you have to eat?" he asked when she merely stood there waiting for the water to boil.

"I require no breakfast, my lord."

Feeling it was his fault she had no appetite,

he asked, "Is there no bread left?"

She went to a basket and peered inside. "We've rolls. Would you care for one, my lord?"

"No, but I will have you eat."

She sat down at the table and tore off a piece of the roll. She chewed it as if it tasted of wood.

"You've no wish for butter or jam?" he inquired.

She shook her head.

"Find yourself some jam," he snapped. Hell and damnation. He should care not if she ate at all. "Make haste," he said when she did not move. "I've not all day."

She quickly complied. "How is..." she began as she spread the jam upon the roll.

"You mean to ask after Mr. Brooke?"

"Yes, my lord."

He looked away. "I know not. I mean to see him when you are done with breakfast."

"May I see him as well?"

He turned back to look at her. He expected she would have wanted to stay behind in the castle and use the opportunity of his absence to run away. Of course he would not allow it, and simply planned to lock her in her quarters before he left.

"There is no need," he replied.

She persisted. "When I was in Forest Blackbourne, I saw bormint growing. In Barbados, I saw my grandmother make a poultice with it to heal a number of injuries that befell those working the plantation."

"I am certain the doctor has his preferred methods."

"May I see him still?"

Her concern irritated him. "You have no desire to see the havoc the wolves did to him."

"Please, my lord!"

Surprised she did not yet relent, he stared at her hard. After what had happened to her last night, she had the capacity to worry about Addison? Was she in love with him?

"You wish to accompany *me* to see Mr. Brooke?" he asked by way of warning. She clearly feared him. Why would she want to spend more time in his company?

She hesitated, and Montague suspected she had changed her mind upon this realization.

"If you would allow it, my lord," she said.

Stunned, he had no response at first. He supposed she had little to lose. If he wanted to, he could ravish her whenever he wished. A trip into the village would not worsen her situation.

"Very well," he grumbled, for Addison would

likely be pleased to see her. "Make yourself presentable. I should like to leave soon."

"Thank you, my lord. I only wish to feed the animals before we leave. I think they might be hungry, as I had not the chance to feed them since yesterday afternoon."

He took himself back upstairs to dress. It was no easy task, shrugging into a form-fitting coat or tying his own neckcloth. Despite his best attempts, his cravat was a sorry sight.

Miss Daliyah looked much improved. She had previously looked a wreck, having lost her mobcap, her tendrils flying everywhere, her face and garments covered in dust and dirt.

Now that she had cleaned herself and donned a new gown, she was rather comely. Montague eyed her from head to toe, his gaze settling at her décolletage. Her cleavage was certainly not without charm.

"You will want a cloak," he said when she drew her flimsy shawl tighter about herself.

"I lost it," she explained.

He gave an exasperated sigh, then told her to come with him to his chambers. Her eyes widened.

"Silly girl, I mean to fetch you a coat," he admonished.

And if I desired to ravish you, I would do it anywhere, he nearly told her. He could take her now, for example. For a fleeting moment, he considered it. But she was scared enough by him. He wanted to explain to her that he was not himself, had not been himself ever since the curse. She saw him as a monster, and rightly so.

She kept her distance from him as they went upstairs to his chambers, as if she had any chance of escaping him should he attempt to take her. After he had a procured a coat for her, she followed him into the stables, where he saddled Aries. After mounting, he pulled Miss Daliyah onto the horse before him. She said nothing as they rode into the village. He could feel the tension in her body. She either did not feel comfortable seated on the horse or to be so near to him. Possibly both. A small part of him wanted to ease her apprehension, but he forced himself not to care. She was but a maid, his next meal if he so chose. A jade who had seduced his brother.

"The bormint!" she cried, twisting her body to point at what they had just passed.

She started to slip from Aries, but he caught her about the waist and held her tightly to him. With her body pressed to him, he caught a strong whiff of her scent. He knew not when she had last bathed, yet after fleeing the castle on foot, battling the wolves, feeding the animals this morning, she still smelled remarkable. Did she not perspire?

The desire to possess her warmed his loins. As if she sensed this, she tried to put space between them, but he continued to hold her tight.

"I take it you've never ridden a horse?" he asked, though he knew the likely answer.

"No, my lord."

They fell back into silence till, several minutes later, she seemed to spot the bormint once more.

"The bormint has potent healing properties, my lord," she pleaded.

He wondered what held her interest more: the bormint or the reprieve from being held so near to him?

He stopped his horse. "Make it quick."

The reprieve, he decided, when she eagerly slid off the horse. He dismounted as well.

Bending over to pick the bormint, she stuffed the plant into her pockets. Though his coat, loose and large upon her, covered her form, he knew the curves she had. It mattered little what she wore, her loveliness did not diminish. Last night, he had speared into her quickly. He had not taken the time to caress her figure. He remembered how extraordinarily smooth and soft her skin was. His hands itched to savor all that her body had to offer.

Though he was eager to see how Addison fared, his brother's condition would likely be no different should a few more minutes pass.

Montague took a step towards Miss Daliyah.

Chapter Sixteen

She felt the chill of his presence upon her neck before she even heard the crunch of his boots upon the ground. As quick as she could, she straightened and turned around. She saw the gleam of desire in his eyes and bolted into the bushes.

Earlier, she had considered resigning herself to her fate. Many in Barbados lived with the constant threat of assault. Though her father had treated her almost as if she were his own, he had allowed his overseers to discipline the slaves as they saw fit. And she had witnessed men who seemed to take satisfaction in mistreating others.

But Lord Blackbourne was unlike any man

she had ever known. He had *fangs*. She had never seen its like in another human. What if he were not human? But that was surely impossible. Aside from sinking his ghastly canines into her, he seemed a man.

An angry man. Or he had been. He had been surprisingly kind to her in letting her sleep in his bed unmolested while he spent the night upon the settee. He had seen that she had breakfast and was warmly clothed. But these tokens of consideration did not mean his anger no longer existed, nor did it absolve him of what he had done. He had intended to hurt her in that dungeon.

Not knowing what he might do next, she could not submit.

And what she feared almost as much as she feared Lord Blackbourne was the response in her own body to his arousal. Over and over she had found herself desperate to join their bodies together. When he had caught her from falling off the horse, she had felt his desire flare, and it seemed to ignite a similar interest in her own body. She thought she might be going mad.

However, she managed only three or four steps before he had grabbed the collar of her coat and yanked her back to him. She stumbled as he pushed her up against a tree, trapping her between it and his body.

"Did you think you could flee from me?" he snarled.

She said nothing. Perhaps now she had to submit. Fighting would undoubtedly make him angrier.

"I own your indenture, Miss Daliyah," he growled. "You belong to me."

"N-Not to do as you please, my lord."

His eyes widened at what he must have regarded as impertinence, but since she had already stoked his wrath, she decided to finish by saying, "You've a right to my services—naught more."

His frown deepened. She thought he might strike her. Instead, he pulled her from the tree and dragged her over to his horse. He mounted, then pulled her up. Though the strange embers of desire still lingered, she was mostly relieved. He continued to hold her tight to him as if to deliberately make her uncomfortable, to convey that he still had the power to do as he wished with her. But she considered it a minor victory that he had chosen not to see through his wicked intentions.

They rode in silence the rest of the way.

"Lord Blackbourne, I did not expect you would be here," the doctor admitted after greeting them outside.

"How does he fare?" Blackbourne demanded as he made his way inside without invitation.

The shorter man hurried to keep stride. "You will want honesty, I wager, as you are a man of courage. The infection set in early. Some of his wounds are too raw for the bandages to be changed."

Daliyah stifled a cry when she saw Mr. Brooke covered in bloody bandages upon the bed. It seemed the wolves had torn at every part of his body. A nurse was in the midst of unwrapping the bandages about his upper arm, revealing a terrible gash around which the flesh had turned a yellowish green.

Looking over, she saw Lord Blackbourne pale.

"I have given what I can to sedate the pain," the doctor continued when Mr. Brooke grimaced.

This was why Lord Blackbourne had been so angry with her, Daliyah realized. She had escaped with minor scratches and bruises while Mr. Brooke lay torn to shreds.

His eyes fluttered open. His gaze focused upon her.

"Miss...Daliyah," he whispered. "You are..."

"Unharmed," Blackbourne filled in.

Unharmed by the wolves, she silently added.

Mr. Brooke started to cough. Lord Blackbourne looked to the dying fire in the hearth.

"Is it cold in here?" he demanded.

Daliyah wanted to nod her head. She looked to the corner of the ceiling where water dripped. Lord Blackbourne followed her gaze.

"What the devil?"

"I meant to have the roof repaired," the doctor said.

Lord Blackbourne grabbed the man by his shirtfront and lifted him off his feet. The nurse gasped.

"You promised me the best care for my br—for Mr. Brooke."

"I d-did," the doctor stammered, "I've spared nothing, but I knew not—I knew not that I would be receiving a patient in such a st-state."

Lord Blackbourne thrust the doctor back onto his feet, but the man stumbled backwards and fell down.

"I will take him back to Castle Blackbourne," Lord Blackbourne declared.

"You mean to move him in this state, my

lord?" asked the doctor as Mr. Brooke coughed.

"I will not leave him here to die of influenza. You will, however, come to Castle Blackbourne each and every day till he is mended. And if I should find your care wanting, you may find another town in which to practice."

Lord Blackbourne stormed out of the room, presumably to find a manner in which to convey Mr. Brooke back to Castle Blackbourne. The man cared a great deal about Mr. Brooke, Daliyah saw. She could feel his desperation and sorrow.

"You there," the doctor said to Daliyah. "Assist with removing the bandages while my nurse procures fresh ones."

She seated herself upon the stool the nurse had occupied. The bandage stuck to the wound and Mr. Brooke grimaced as she attempted to peel it away.

"Such a fuss over a servant," the doctor grumbled as he and his nurse walked out the door.

"Were not a great number of the Blackbourne servants dismissed?" the nurse asked. "And I heard two or three went missing."

"Little wonder if his lordship behaves more like a brute than a gentleman."

"I've never seen the dark maid before," the nurse remarked before their voices faded.

Mr. Brooke continued to gaze upon Daliyah. "I'm so glad—"

"Shhh," she pleaded. "If words be needed, it is only I who ought speak to beg your forgiveness."

"Nay, you must not—"

"We will talk of this later."

With the bandages removed, she washed the wound as carefully as she could. The nurse returned with new bandages. Daliyah stood aside. She felt sick with guilt. It had been a grave and foolish mistake to run from Blackbourne when she did.

The nurse stoked the fire, and Daliyah sat at Mr. Brooke's bedside till Lord Blackbourne arrived, having secured a carriage.

The doctor proceeded to explain the many efforts he had made on Mr. Brooke's behalf and how the nurse came highly recommended. Lord Blackbourne appeared to listen with half an ear as he approached Mr. Brooke's bed. A muscle along his jaw tightened.

"He has a small fever," Daliyah informed him.

Lord Blackbourne looked sharply at the

doctor.

"Which is why I kept the room on the colder side," the doctor explained, "to cool the fever."

"My grandmother believed—"

She stopped speaking when the doctor glared at her. Realizing she ought not challenge the man, she remained silent.

After Mr. Brooke had been moved into the carriage, Daliyah joined him in the vehicle, leaving Lord Blackbourne to ride Aries back to the castle. The doctor and nurse followed in a gig.

Back home, Lord Blackbourne had Mr. Brooke installed in a room upstairs. The doctor looked over Mr. Brooke and asked if Lord Blackbourne wanted the nurse to remain behind.

"That will not be necessary," Lord Blackbourne said. "Miss Daliyah will be caring for Mr. Brooke in your absence. Pray, instruct her as to what she must do."

The doctor glanced over at Daliyah with misgiving. "Are you certain, my lord? She is a housemaid, is she not?"

"And highly competent. When you are done, you and your nurse are dismissed."

Accepting his lordship's orders, the doctor

proceeded to describe to Daliyah how often the bandages would need changing, his thoughts on how to keep the fever down, and how she had to keep a diligent eye on the infection.

"If needed, I will bleed him tomorrow to address the fever," the doctor said. "I might also make use of leeches to draw out the infection."

Daliyah could not wait for the doctor to be gone. After he departed, she took out the bormint she had plucked from the forest. With it, she made a poultice, adding oregano, garlic, and honey.

With Lord Blackbourne's assistance, they removed Mr. Brooke's garments, darkened and crusted with blood. She wiped him clean as best she could, then gently undid the bandages to apply the poultice.

"Did Mr. Thomson give you that?" Lord Blackbourne asked.

"It is the bormint, my lord."

"Are you certain your concoction will not worsen the wounds?"

"My grandmother used it often back in Barbados. On the plantation, slaves suffered all manner of injuries, from severed arms to burnt flesh from the boilers."

"Your grandmother was a nurse?"

"A healer. They all sought her out. And I have helped her since my childhood."

Lord Blackbourne did not appear convinced, but he nodded for her to continue and assisted with the new bandages.

When she was done, he told her, "You will take the room adjoining this one, that you may see to Mr. Brooke more easily."

He turned to take his leave.

"My lord," she blurted. When he turned back around, she continued, "I will do all that I can to care for Mr. Brooke. If I had not run out into the forest, he would have been spared all this. But it would ease me much if you refrained from...imposing yourself upon me."

His countenance hardened. He turned toward the door. "We shall see."

Chapter Seventeen

The clock above the mantel in his chambers ticked past midnight. Montague had slept but a few hours in the early morning hours yesterday, but he remained restless tonight. Mr. Thomson seemed less than adequate, and though he did not doubt that Miss Daliyah would care for Addison with diligence, he hoped his confidence in her was not misplaced.

He had felt her stare upon him often today, and it was not always because she was watchful of what he might do, like a deer alerted to predators. He was glad that she had not fallen into hysterics, as others had done when he bared his fangs. Like the others, she had struggled and succumbed. This time, however, she had not taken days to recover.

Despite her fear, she had continued in her duties without fail, asking him when he wished to take supper. He had declined any sustenance and told her to cook what she wished for herself. He had thought to request her assistance in removing his riding boots, but he worried that her nearness would flame his ardor. Addison should be her primary concern.

Deciding to look in on his brother, Montague walked into Addison's room. Addison was asleep. Beside him, Miss Daliyah sat upon the floor with her head resting against the side of the bed, also asleep. Montague thought to move her, but his touch might frighten her, which would then disturb Addison. Finding a blanket, he placed it upon Miss Daliyah. He placed a fresh log upon the fire and wandered downstairs.

Without thought, he found himself in a drawing room. As children, when they played hide-and-seek, Addison liked to hide behind the curtains in this room.

Montague went to the sideboard. Since the curse, he cared little for libations of any kind, but tonight, he wanted the numbness that wine could provide. He decided to pour himself a claret.

He thought of Miss Daliyah's request to him. Given her usual deferential manners, her nerve had surprised him. She did not understand that he had little control over his desires. She did not know what he suffered. And now his infernal curse may have doomed the one person he cared about above all others.

Soon after the curse, he had bid Addison to leave him to his misery, but when his brother had refused, he selfishly accepted Addison's decision. He wanted Addison with him, and now his brother would pay the price with his life.

"Bloody damnation!"

Montague downed the claret, then threw the glass at the wall where it shattered and fell to the floor. Grabbing another glass, he poured himself more of the claret, though he relished the wine as much as he would drinking sand.

How could he have allowed this to happen to Addison? Why did he not have the courage to end his miserable existence? Doing so would have spared his brother. Perhaps it would have been better if he had consumed all of Miss Daliyah that first night. Granted, he would have had to continue to find new victims, but that would have saved Addison. He would not have been torn asunder by those wolves.

Tightening his grip, Montague crushed the glass he held. The shards cut into his hand.

"My lord!" came a gasp from the threshold.

It was Miss Daliyah. She rushed to him and gasped once more at beholding his bloody hand. Setting down her candle, she took his hand and pulled out the pieces of glass.

"Leave it be," he grumbled.

But she continued to pick at the pieces. Removing one of her pins, she used it to pry the smaller shards from his flesh.

When done, she said, "If you would wait here, my lord, I will fetch bandages."

While she was gone, Montague poured a third glass, then a fourth, though he knew the claret would have no effect. The curse had deprived him of all relief.

Miss Daliyah returned with bandages and proceeded to wrap his hand.

"Why do you do this?" he asked.

"Because you are hurt, my lord."

"You could have passed this room without my knowing and left me to bleed."

She said nothing.

"Why did you not?" he pressed.

She looked up from the bandages. "I saw that you were in pain."

"Would that not have pleased you, after how I had treated you?"

"I have seen too much pain and suffering to ever take pleasure in it."

"Then you are a better person than most," he said with some bitterness.

"It is kind of you to care so greatly for Mr. Brooke. Not many masters would grieve so for their servants."

With a groan, Montague sat down. He placed a hand over his eyes. "Addison is more than a servant to me. He is my half-brother."

Why he chose to divulge this to Miss Daliyah when he had never spoken of it to anyone, he knew not. Perhaps the claret was having an influence after all.

She said nothing at first. "You are both fortunate to have such a devoted brother."

"It is because of his devotion that he lies upstairs, possibly at Death's door," he croaked.

"I believe the Good Book says in Psalms, 'Praise the Lord, my soul, and forget not all his benefits—who forgives all your sins and heals all your diseases.'"

Montague leaped to his feet and stormed away. "Quote not the Bible to me! That book is useless to one as cursed as me."

"How are you cursed, my lord?"

He whirled around to face her, taking in her large, innocent eyes, her delectable female form, her beautiful throat. A part of him wanted to drain her and send them all to a fiery grave.

"You had best leave, Miss Daliyah," he advised.

She must have sensed his fiendish thoughts, for she made no protest and took her leave without word. He watched her depart, then sank back into his chair.

If there was no hope for Addison, he cared not what happened to anyone, including himself.

Chapter Eighteen

O *ne as cursed as me.*
Daliyah fell asleep to these words upon the settee in Mr. Brooke's room. In her slumber, she relived the attack of the wolves as well as her night in the dungeon with Lord Blackbourne. At the end, Lord Blackbourne merged with a wolf. Sharp fangs threatened to pierce her neck.

She woke with a start, her heart racing. What was she doing here? She ought to flee at the earliest chance, during the day when the wolves were gone.

But then she looked upon Mr. Brooke. He needed her.

Rising from the settee, she went to him and touched his forehead. He still had a fever. Last night, he had also developed chills. She had kept the fire steady in the hearth throughout the night and refilled the warming pan several times.

Gazing upon his features, she saw once more the similarities between Mr. Brooke and Lord Blackbourne. At first glance, they could look quite different to many, but they had similar lines in the face. Lord Blackbourne's jaw was more square, perhaps filled out by more years, but the shape of the brows and the nose were nearly identical.

That Lord Blackbourne clearly loved his brother gave her some solace. She had felt his pain, his grief last night as she bound his hand. She wondered if the men shared a mother or a father? Their situations in life differed tremendously, as did their dispositions: one aloof and capable of wrath, the other friendly and kind.

As gently as she could, she unwrapped the bandages from Mr. Brooke's arms, shoulders, and legs. She would need assistance to unwrap the bandages about his ribs. After cleaning the wounds, she applied more of the poultice and wrapped new bandages about him. Taking the blanket Lord Blackbourne must have placed upon her last night, she laid it over Mr. Brooke, then went downstairs to the kitchen to make herself coffee. She supposed if Lord Blackbourne needed her, he would ring for her, but she prepared a breakfast for him should he wake hungry. She had not seen him eat or drink all day yesterday save for the claret.

She took a tea she made from various herbs to Mr. Brooke. Though he was greatly fatigued, he managed to drink a cup with her assistance. Afterwards, she tended to her chores for an hour before the doctor arrived.

"How fares Mr. Brooke?" he asked.

"I think his fever slightly worse than yesterday," she replied.

"Then we should bleed him."

"After he has lost blood already?"

He glared at her.

She looked down. "I shall fetch Lord Blackbourne for you."

Leaving the doctor, she went to his lordship's chambers and knocked upon the door. She knocked again when there was no response. She was about to knock a third time when the door opened. Lord Blackbourne, in only a banyan draped over his nightshirt, looked quite disheveled and bleary eyed, as if he had just woken.

"What is it?" he grumbled.

"Mr. Thomson is here," she answered. "He means to...bleed Mr. Brooke."

"What of it?"

"I wonder that Mr. Brooke has blood to spare, given he has already bled so much."

Lord Blackbourne raised a brow. "Are you purporting to be a doctor, Miss Daliyah?"

"I saw it done once to the plantation overseer. He failed to improve. In the end, he did not survive."

"You know not that the bleeding had naught to do with the man's death. Nor are you a doctor."

"Could not Mr. Thomson wait a day to see if the fever will retreat? My grandmother believed fevers could be helpful in warding off malignant spirits."

"Malignant spirits?" Lord Blackbourne scoffed... but then he paused, as if recalling a memory. "I will see the doctor when I am dressed."

He closed the door, and Daliyah returned to Mr. Brooke's room.

"My lord," the doctor greeted when Lord Blackbourne appeared a few minutes later.

"Your maid has done an adequate job with the bandages. The infection upon the arm appears to have receded, but as the fever is still present, I think we can release some of the heat through the letting of blood."

"Are you certain that will improve the fever?" Lord Blackbourne asked.

"It is a common remedy for fever, my lord."

"How often have you bled a man with fever and seen improvement?"

"The effects are not instant. Sometimes, several bleedings must be attempted."

"But they have all been successful in the end?"

"Perhaps not *all*..."

"Are there just as many times when the fever has resolved itself without bleeding?" Lord Blackbourne inquired.

"Perhaps, but I believe the bleeding will hasten the fever to depart."

"What if we were to wait till the morrow?"

"Fevers can kill, my lord."

"You say the infection is less?"

"A wound or two appears improved, yes."

Lord Blackbourne knit his brow in thought. "Let us see if the fever similarly improves."

"If you wish, my lord. I would also advise this

room be kept cooler to counter the fever."

Risking the doctor's ire once more, Daliyah said, "Mr. Brooke had the chills last night."

"That makes little sense," Mr. Thomson returned. "Mr. Brooke clearly has a fever. His body has too much heat." Looking to Lord Blackbourne, Mr. Thomson asked, "My nurse can be made available to you, my lord. She is quite practiced in the care of patients who have sustained great injuries."

Unlike your maid, the doctor seemed to silently add when he looked in Daliyah's direction.

"I will let you know if I choose to accept your offer," Lord Blackbourne replied.

Mr. Thomson soon departed with the promise that he would return the following day. When the doctor had left, Lord Blackbourne turned to her.

"Your notions had best prove true," he said.

"Yes, my lord."

He pressed his lips into a grim line before saying, "I take it you are not fool enough to risk my wrath should you be wrong."

"I wish only for your brother's health," she replied. "His injuries already weigh upon my conscience."

He seemed satisfied with her response and went to the bed to examine his brother.

"Would you care for breakfast, my lord?" she asked. "I made eggs and toast."

"No."

"Shall I change your bandages?"

He looked down at his hand. "Very well."

He took a seat, and she knelt before him to unwrap the bandages. His hand was cool to the touch.

"You heal quickly, my lord," she said, marveling that some of his cuts had started to close with no signs of infection.

With fresh linen, she began to wrap his hand, conscious of his gaze upon her. Her pulse quickened. She could feel the tug of his desire. Would he dare make an attempt upon her with his brother lying but a few feet away?

Chapter Nineteen

Montague stared at her as she wound the bandage about his hand. She was warm to the touch. As if she knew the temptation rising in him, she quickened her pace and seemed to avoid his gaze. Even after he had deliberately attempted to make her miserable, she still looked after him. It was the obvious duty of a servant to make him breakfast, but she need not have offered to change his bandages. She could have hoped he would not notice he needed fresh linen. The doctor hadn't.

Montague could not decide if he admired her kindness of heart or found her pathetic.

Regardless, with her kneeling so near to him, his appetite for flesh reared its head. His gaze fixed upon her mouth, so much more plump than

Miss Cameron's. He could not decide if he liked Miss Daliyah's lips, but he did want to kiss them. All he had to do was lower his head to take her mouth with his. Would she submit or would she fight?

With his blood pounding in his veins, he stood up abruptly and took his leave before she had finished bandaging his hand. He had not promised her that he would not ravish her, but he would not do it before Addison.

That damn maid had better be right with her bormint and objections to bleeding.

After shaving himself, he changed into his riding attire. He wondered if she would attempt to escape while he was gone. She seemed genuine in her concern for Addison, which suggested that she would not abandon him, but would she truly put his welfare above her own?

If she did attempt to flee, Montague was certain he could hunt her down, and he would not be so kind after he had gone through the trouble of finding her.

Passing by his brother's room, he saw Miss Daliyah holding Addison, gently persuading him to drink the tea she held. She had spent the night at his side, just as Addison had once spent the night at her side.

Proceeding to the stables, where he saddled Aries, Montague rode his steed into a gallop. He rode for an hour. The activity settled the disquiet in his body better than the claret had. When he returned, he half expected to find Miss Daliyah gone. Instead, he spotted her outside, washing bed linen.

"Mr. Brooke perspires a great deal between his chills," she explained. "I have changed his bedclothes twice today. Shall I see to your horse, my lord?"

"No," he replied. He did not realize how glad he would be that she hadn't fled till he saw her.

"Will you want to take tea, my lord?"

He was about to decline, then changed his mind. "If you will take it with me."

He saw her reluctance.

"I will have tea," he rephrased. "In the study."

After stabling Aries, he changed out of his riding clothes and went downstairs into the study, which was, comfortably, not as bright as the drawing room.

Miss Daliyah set down the tea with biscuits, brown bread, and roast pork.

"Stay," he said when she turned to leave. "Sit."

She hesitated but complied.

"Have the tea you poured," he ordered.

"But what of you, my lord?" she asked.

"You may procure me another cup later."

She rose. "Or I can fetch another cup."

"Sit. Do as you're told."

She sat back down and picked up the cup. He watched her take a small sip.

"Did you have lunch?"

"There was much to do."

"Then you will eat now."

When she made no move, he filled a plate and placed it upon her lap. "Eat. I will not have you fainting from hunger and rendered unable to care for Addison."

At that, she began to nibble at the food. He remained standing as he watched her.

"Will you not require sustenance too, my lord?" she asked.

He eyed her delicious throat for a moment. "I can see to my own needs."

She picked up a biscuit.

"You were in Barbados, were you?" he asked.

"Yes, my lord."

"Were you born there?"

"Yes, my lord."

"Who were your parents? How came you to

have such refined speech and the ability to write?"

"I was raised in the great house," she answered. "The master of the house was kind to me and took me in."

"Who were your parents?"

"My mother was a slave. She perished from scarlet fever when I was young. I was raised by my grandmother."

"But you were born free?"

"I was granted manumission."

"And your father?"

She chewed slowly. He eyed her more closely. Her features and her complexion differed somewhat from the darker slaves he had seen.

"Was he the master of the house?" he guessed.

She did not look at him.

"How are you now an indentured servant?" he asked.

"When my father took ill, his wife wanted him back in England, that he could be cared for by the best English doctors. I wished to be with him, but I had not the funds for the voyage. In exchange for passage to England, I became an indentured servant."

"And where is your father now?"

"Not long after I had arrived in England, I learned that he had passed."

He shifted in discomfort. "A most unfortunate circumstance."

"Not as unfortunate as those whom I left behind in Barbados," she said quietly.

"Still, you must pity yourself greatly."

"I pity those who have not their freedom."

"Does that include yourself?"

She met his gaze. "I have the promise of freedom."

He recalled Addison telling him she had been on the verge of purchasing the remainder of her indenture from her previous employer.

He changed the subject. "Have you any siblings?"

"My father and his wife had two daughters. They live here in England."

"Have you met them?"

"They would not receive me."

He said nothing more till she finished her cup of tea and set down her plate upon the table. "Why did you not attempt to flee when I was away riding?"

"Mr. Brooke suffered his injuries for my sake. I owe it to him to see to his care."

"And that is all?"

"My lord?"

"You are either brave to remain behind, or stupid."

She rose. "If you will, my lord, I should see to Mr. Brooke." Without waiting for him to reply, she started to depart.

Shooting out his arm, he stopped her just as she passed him.

"I've not dismissed you yet, Miss Daliyah."

With his hand at her waist, he pulled her closer to him and heard the breath escape from her parted lips. With his other hand, he clasped her chin and turned her face toward his. He took a deep breath of her scent. The blood in him warmed. How had she become even more entrancing? Was this how she had ensnared his brother?

He eyed her lips and smelled her apprehension. But was there more than just fear? Her bosom rose and fell with short breaths.

"My lord, your brother requires another application of the bormint," she whispered.

Though he wanted to taste her lips more than he wanted to feed upon her, he released her. He watched her scurry away. It was only a matter of time, he decided, before he would plumb the depths between those supple lips.

Chapter Twenty

Lord Blackbourne had withheld himself at least thrice when she was sure he had wanted to ravish her, but how much longer could he refrain?

Daliyah saw his need plainly. Distressingly, she *also* felt his need. But even if he had desires that tested his forbearance, he had not the right to impose himself upon her.

Law and convention, however, said otherwise.

All the more reason for her to secure her freedom, she thought to herself, that she need not live under the tyranny of those who held mastery in this world.

Back in Mr. Brooke's bedchamber, she applied more of the bormint. He grunted and grimaced with her every touch.

The rest of the day, she saw little of Lord Blackbourne. When she asked if he wanted supper, he said she could leave a tray in his chambers.

By night, she felt weary and longed for a bath. But she wanted to ensure the fire in Mr. Brooke's bedchamber remained strong, despite what the doctor had recommended.

When she was done stoking the fire, she heard Mr. Brooke whisper her name. She went to him immediately.

"Thank God you've…" he whispered.

She felt his forehead and below his jaw to find him still burning with fever. He grasped her hand.

"Would you like more tea?" she asked.

He closed his eyes and seemed to fade into sleep, though he continued to clasp her hand tightly. She attempted to disengage, but he did not release her. She decided to remain a little while. When he went into deeper slumber, his grip would relax.

But she fell into deep sleep as well.

When she blinked her eyes open, her hand was still in Mr. Brooke's. And standing at the threshold was Lord Blackbourne. How long had he been there? she wondered.

He sauntered over and gave her his candle. "Go. Retire to your chambers. I will watch over him tonight."

She slid her hand from Mr. Brooke's and curtsied before taking her leave. Still tired, she collapsed into her bed as soon as she removed her slippers.

Nightmares of wolves continued to haunt her, startling her awake in the middle of the night. She sat up in bed, her pulse racing, and looked about, worried that there were wolves in her room. But there was only the darkness and silence.

Putting on her slippers, she went into Mr. Brooke's room. The fire had weakened. Mr. Brooke remained asleep and on the settee sat Lord Blackbourne, awake. The room felt heavy with his agony. She felt Mr. Brooke's fever and the bedclothes to see if they were dry.

"I'm the reason he lies there," Lord Blackbourne murmured. "Because I'm too cowardly to put an end to my curse. If only he cared more for himself, he would not suffer so."

She was quiet for a moment before asking, "Is it not a blessing to have his love and devotion?"

He scoffed and replied bitterly, "Not for him."

"I'm sure Mr. Brooke would consider your love and devotion a blessing."

"My father had intended to cast him out. Addison was, granted, a bastard child, but he was nonetheless my father's son. I persuaded our father not to. Had I known then what I now know, I would have let my father see his intentions through."

Lord Blackbourne let his head fall against the wall behind him. "I have cried a hundred tears for myself, yet, as my brother lies there in tatters, mayhap days from Death, my eyes are bone dry."

She glanced over at Mr. Brooke. "I believe he will mend."

"You think I should place great stock in the words of a housemaid, the daughter of a slave?"

"I sense his strength, his determination."

His lordship snorted.

"If you believe my thoughts unworthy of regard, why did you allow me to use the bormint? Why did you not agree with Mr. Thomson to bleed your brother?"

"In truth, I've not the foggiest. Perhaps because I've not the greatest confidence in Mr. Thomson."

Silence fell between them till she said, "If you

wish to sleep in your own chambers, I can stay the rest of the night with Mr. Brooke."

"He is my brother and my responsibility. I have brought this suffering upon him."

One might think he said as much because it was he who had caused her to take flight. Mr. Brooke would not have encountered her in the forest otherwise. But Daliyah intuited that Lord Blackbourne referred to something else.

"You know a little of suffering," Lord Blackbourne said to her, "and the unfairness of a world set against you, of a God who has abandoned you."

Did he claim to suffer himself? What could a man endowed with his wealth, position, strength, and features suffer from?

"The Bible says 'He will not fail you or abandon you, so do not lose courage or be afraid.'"

"I told you I've no use for bloody scripture."

"Your pardon, my lord."

"Pray tell you are not a devout Christian."

"My father went to church sparingly, but I was told Englishmen find comfort in the Bible."

"Nothing can comfort the likes of me."

They became silent once more.

"Go to bed, Miss Daliyah," Lord Blackbourne

bid.

Obeying, she left. As she settled into her bed, she considered that he had twice mentioned a curse. Was that the cause of his suffering? What manner of curse could his be?

She fell asleep without any answers to her queries.

In the morning, she went first to see Mr. Brooke. Lord Blackbourne lay upon the settee asleep. Placing her hand upon Mr. Brooke's brow, she felt he did not burn as much as before. She felt the bedclothes and found them dry.

Lord Blackbourne stirred. Seeing her expression, he asked, "What is it?"

"His fever has broken," she answered.

Walking over, he felt for himself.

Mr. Brooke opened his eyes. "Montague." Seeing her presence, he corrected himself. "My lord."

"I confessed the truth to her. She knows we are brothers," Lord Blackbourne said.

Mr. Brooke appeared surprised.

Lord Blackbourne looked to her. "But she has no reason to speak of this to anyone."

She nodded in acknowledgement.

"Half-brothers," Mr. Brooke added.

"I will fetch some tea for you," she said, happy

to see him much improved.

"That won't—"

"I will humor no protests," Lord Blackbourne interrupted. "You will do as she says. And you will rest. Nothing more."

She saw the weight of agony lifted from his countenance. When she returned with the tea, Lord Blackbourne sat at his brother's side while Mr. Brooke, still weak, had his eyes closed. He stirred when she set the tray down and eyed the teapot with misgiving.

"That the same tea you had me drink before?" he inquired.

"It is," she answered. "My grandmother used to make it."

She poured a cup while Lord Blackbourne assisted his brother into a more upright position.

"Will the tea help with the pain?" Mr. Brooke asked.

"A little."

As he had his right shoulder and his left arm wrapped in bandages, she held the cup for him. He sipped the tea. From his expression, he clearly found the taste wanting. Lord Blackbourne smirked.

"I dare you to finish a cup," Mr. Brooke returned despite his weakness. After he had finished as much as he could tolerate, he lay back down. "How long have I been rendered useless?"

"It matters not," Lord Blackbourne replied. "Miss Daliyah has been more than capable."

Mr. Brooke glanced between the two of them, his brow furrowed.

Lord Blackbourne said to her, "You should partake of some breakfast before you begin your chores, and Mr. Thomson should be here shortly."

Mr. Brooke had closed his eyes once more, and Daliyah took herself back downstairs to the kitchen. The doctor arrived at the same hour as yesterday, this time with his nurse. Daliyah opened the door for them and followed upstairs to Mr. Brooke's room.

"I thought you may wish to reconsider the services of my nurse," Mr. Thomson said.

"I think not," Lord Blackbourne said. "Mr. Brooke is already showing signs of improvement. The fever is all but gone."

"Indeed?" Mr. Thomson went over to inspect Mr. Brooke. "This bodes well, but let us see how the infection fares."

He had his nurse undo the bandages.

"Remarkable," he commented. "I've never

seen an infection retreat so quickly."

Lord Blackbourne raised his brows and glanced over to where Daliyah stood. "A poultice of bormint was applied to his wounds."

"Bormint? I've never heard of such a thing."

"Apparently, the plant grows in Forest Blackbourne."

"It is hard to believe a mere plant can have such wondrous results. The plant would need to have magical properties." The doctor pushed his spectacles up his nose and looked again at Mr. Brooke's wound. "It is as if this has been the work of— But, in truth, I do not believe in..."

"Believe in what?" Lord Blackbourne prodded.

"Witchcraft."

Chapter Twenty One

Addison woke with his body still throbbing with pain. It seemed a thousand needles pierced his arms, shoulders, legs, and ribs. The wolves would have torn him to shreds had Montague not arrived when he did.

Addison attempted to sit upright, prompting his brother, who stood staring out the window, to turn around. As the move caused his aches to swell, Addison settled back into the pillows.

"Miss Daliyah—was she hurt?" he asked of Montague.

"Barely. I thought the wolves ready to tear her asunder, but it seemed they hesitated," his brother replied.

"It was fortunate you came. I tried..."

"It was foolhardy to think that you could best

those wolves," Montague scolded, "but on horseback, you might have outrun them."

"And leave Miss Daliyah to perish?"

His brother narrowed his eyes. "You would sacrifice your life for hers?"

"Is she not your only known hope?"

Montague appeared chastened and said nothing for a moment before asking, "If not for my sake, then you would not have attempted to save her?"

Addison made no reply, though he knew the answer.

"What did you do to her?" he asked. When his brother did not respond, Addison added, "What compelled her to run into the cursed forest? She knew it to be infested with fiendish wolves."

"I did what the curse would have me do," Montague growled. "She saw my fangs this time."

Addison closed his eyes and roared a silent oath. If only he had not taken as long as he had in the village! He could not imagine the fright Miss Daliyah must have experienced.

He opened his eyes and pinned his stare on Montague. "And since then?"

"She fears me still, but her desire to care for you seems paramount at the moment."

It was not the answer Addison sought.

"Have you touched her since she fled?" he specified.

"What does it matter if I did?" Montague snapped. "I can tell you there were many times I was tempted, but I did not. For your sake."

Addison looked away, vexed that Miss Daliyah had to deal with Montague by herself.

"You ought not worry of her," Montague said. "I know better than to feed too much upon her. In truth, I have not felt the thirst for blood as much in the past few days."

"And what of your other appetite?"

Montague said nothing. Addison wondered how much of *that* was the result of the curse or his brother's own carnal cravings.

"For your sake," Montague replied, "I have attempted to refrain as much as possible."

"Where is she now?"

"Tending the vegetables in the garden. I have kept an eye on her, should she attempt to flee again."

"Has she?"

"Attempted to flee? I think not. I went on a ride with Aries yesterday and expected to find her gone when I returned but found her washing your bedclothes."

Addison sighed with misery. After all that she had been through, she remained steadfast in her chores and devoted to tending to him.

And I deserve none of her efforts.

"She is remarkable," Addison said.

"I suppose she is...uncommon," Montague agreed in a low voice. He went to the tray of tea and poured a cup. "Here. Drink the tea she made."

"That tea is most foul."

"You will drink it nonetheless."

After Addison had finished the tea with Montague's assistance, he said, "I heard the conversation with the doctor. Do you truly think it witchcraft?"

"Perhaps her kind practice arts we know not of. You are mending with strange speed."

"But then, do you think Miss Daliyah a witch?"

"Till my curse, I would not have believed in the existence of witches. Some of the research I have read asserts that persons are born witches, while others believe that it is possible for any person to learn the craft."

"If Miss Daliyah were a witch, she might be able to reverse your curse."

"It has become *our* curse," Montague

lamented. "But if Miss Daliyah were a witch, she is either a poor one or oblivious, else she would have placed her own curse upon me or done better to protect herself."

"True."

Addison closed his eyes. The *tête-à-tête* with his brother was draining.

"I would sooner consider her an angel," he murmured.

His words seemed to disconcert Montague, who turned away. Addison wondered if there was more his brother withheld from telling him? He willed himself to mend as soon as possible. As much as he loved his brother, he could not fully trust Montague. He told himself it was because of the curse, which would change even the most stalwart and pure of men. It was a belief Addison had to hold onto.

Chapter Twenty Two

While his brother slept, Montague went in search of Miss Daliyah. He would not allow her out of his sight for more than twenty minutes at a time. Thus, if he should find her missing, he could go in search of her easily enough.

He found her outside attempting to chop wood. She wielded the heavy ax awkwardly and chipped rather than split a wood block.

"Give the ax here," he commanded after he had walked up to her.

Taking it, he chopped the block in half.

"I take it Mr. Brooke is resting?" she asked.

He nodded, then picked up another block of wood to chop. "I had him drink more of your tea."

"It will hasten his recovery."

"How much wood do you desire?"

She indicated the two large baskets upon the ground.

"You think you can carry both of those?" he inquired dubiously.

"I would not have filled them to the brim, and I would have carried them one at a time."

He removed his coat and chopped enough wood to fill both baskets, which he then carried into the castle for her.

"Thank you, my lord," she said. "I should not have accepted your assistance had I more strength or skill for chopping wood."

He shook his head. "You would have attempted all this yourself if I had not come along?"

"Well, there is only Mr. Brooke and myself, my lord."

"What more do you have to do?"

"The horses need to be fed and the cow milked."

"I know not how to milk a cow, but I can feed the horses."

"My lord, I could not ask you to—"

"You are not asking. Nor am I offering. It is an order."

"In truth, I rather like feeding the horses."

Relenting, he decided to assist her instead. In the stables, she greeted Aries first.

"Careful," Montague reminded her. "That cantankerous animal will sooner bite your hand off than allow you to touch him."

But the steed allowed her approach and remained passive while she stroked his mane.

"Horses are such magnificent creatures," she said as she smiled at Aries.

She spent time with each of the five horses before turning to him and saying, "We never went in search of Mr. Brooke's horse."

"That horse knew its way back to Castle Blackbourne," Montague said. "If he has not returned, then it is likely—"

He stopped when her eyes grew wide with concern.

"Should we not make an attempt to find the poor thing?" she asked.

"It would be a waste of time."

"Perhaps the creature is too frightened to know its way."

"Do you not have a great many chores, Miss Daliyah, not the least of which includes caring for my brother?"

"I do, but some, like the candle dipping or the dishes, I could do when everyone is retired for the night."

"And when would you sleep?" he returned, noticing the shadows beneath her eyes. "I will not have you spending time on a fruitless search when you could be attending more urgent tasks."

She looked down in disappointment.

Though he had no interest in combing the forest for an animal he could replace, he did not like seeing her downcast look. "I will go in search of the horse," he grumbled.

She immediately brightened.

He eyed her warily and warned, "Mind you, I will not be long."

He helped her saddle Aries. Though he was not in his riding clothes, he did not want to spend more time than necessary on what he deemed a waste of effort.

And he was right.

He found the carcass of the horse, though most of the flesh had been torn from the bones, not far from where the wolves had attacked Addison and Miss Daliyah.

Upon returning, he found Miss Daliyah standing over a large kettle of scalding-hot water, which she used to melt tallow. Her skin glistened with perspiration. She wiped her brow before skimming the tallow and putting it through a sieve atop another pot.

Unaware of his gaze, she took a handkerchief to wipe the moisture that had accumulated in her cleavage. She wiped her brow once more and pulled at her garments, which clung to her. She stifled a yawn before dipping the wicks into the tallow.

Montague silently cursed. There was no reason to pity her. She was doing nothing more than what was expected of a servant, he told himself. Nonetheless, Addison would have praised her industry or rewarded her with another silly bouquet of flowers.

Montague cleared his throat. She looked up and knew, possibly from his expression, that he did not come bearing good news.

"You found the horse?" she guessed.

"I did."

She looked down, visibly saddened.

Not knowing what more to say, he told her he would draw a bath.

"Once I am done with the candles—" she began.

"You look ready to fall over from weariness," he interrupted, "and as likely to spill water all over the place."

He filled two large buckets of water, which he

carried upstairs. He started a fire in her chambers and poured the water into a large pot above the flames. After returning for more water, he had filled the pot. Once the water was heated, he transferred it into a bathtub.

Till today, he had never drawn a bath before, had never chopped wood. Addison would be shocked.

"Your bath is ready in your chambers," he said to Miss Daliyah as she was hanging the last of the candles to dry.

"My lord?"

"When was the last time you bathed?"

Her brow furrowed as she seemed to count the days in her head.

As he truly did not care what her answer would be, he said, "I expect cleanliness among Blackbourne servants. If you are done with the candles, you are to see to your bath."

With his stare, he dared her to protest. She did not.

After she went upstairs, he went in search of better garments for her. The prior maids at Blackbourne had left little behind. He found a gown from a plump maid he had devoured soon after his curse, but the garment would be too large upon Miss Daliyah. Remembering that his father had not gifted away all his mother's clothes after she had passed, he went into her former chambers, where he found petticoats, chemises, corsets, stockings, and a variety of gowns.

Taking an armful of garments, he returned to Miss Daliyah's chambers.

She gasped at his entrance.

Thinking only to deposit the clothes he had found, he had not considered she would be in the bath already. He stopped in his tracks. She sat in the water with one arm crossed over her bosom, holding the opposite shoulder. She drew up her knees, though he had already glimpsed her torso. Her figure was more beguiling than he remembered. He supposed he had been too much in the throes of his appetites to appreciate her form before.

A gentleman would shield his eyes and take his leave. But he had never been the best of gentlemen *before* the curse. After the curse, the thought of being a gentleman was laughable. If he remained, however, he might undo any goodwill he had built by treating her better.

He set the garments down upon a nearby settee. "These are yours."

She glanced at them. "But they are too fine to

work in!"

"What does it matter? They belonged to my mother and are of no use to anyone now."

"I have my own garments, my lord."

"The soiled one you perspired in while dipping candles, and the other, torn, with blood and dirt? I would have you look more presentable."

At that, she had no response. He continued to stare at her, unable to move himself. He wished for a way to satisfy his appetites without inflicting harm upon her. But such wishes served no purpose. Guilt served no purpose. A sixmonth into his curse, he had ceased to care. It was not his fault he had been made a monster.

He sauntered closer.

Chapter Twenty Three

Daliyah had nothing to protect herself with, not even clothes to cover herself. She curled her body tighter, shrinking herself, averting her gaze, for she could only hope that he would choose to restrain himself. But could he? She sensed a terrible war within him.

Daring to look at him, she saw the conflict in his eyes. Arousal flamed in his gaze, which fell to her bosom, but there was also torment and a touch of loathing. His was no simple need to assert dominance or satiate the cravings of the flesh. She was reminded of what he had said last night about suffering. What was the nature of his suffering?

"I will see to my brother now," he said

abruptly and whirled about on his heels.

She watched him depart in relief. She had thought for certain he would ravish her. He had withheld himself, though it was clear that was what he had desired to do. He was not without some semblance of conscience or kindness. She felt poorly for him. For all that he possessed, his ability to seize whatever he desired, he was miserable. Tortured.

She finished her bath and, drying herself, looked over the garments Lord Blackbourne had set down. The gown, befitting the wardrobe of a lady, was made of silk brocade. The quilted petticoats were edged with lace. Daliyah had never worn such finery in her life. She pulled the chemise over her. How soft it felt! And the silk stockings, too.

Taking up the corset, she frowned. It laced in the back. She would require assistance, but there were no other maids about. She considered pinning the frock to itself, but that would require more pins and might damage the material. While she contemplated what she could do, Lord Blackbourne returned.

She dropped the corset in surprise.

"My brother is asleep," he said. "Perhaps you could make more of your tea for him when he wakes."

Standing in only the chemise and stockings, she only nodded.

He picked up the corset from the floor and handed it to her.

"Thank you, my lord, but I will wear mine own."

"That is nonsense."

"This corset laces in back, my lord, which I cannot do on my own."

"I know how to lace a bloody corset."

She supposed she ought not be surprised. He likely had experience *unlacing* them.

Taking the corset, which was partially laced, she stepped into it. Lord Blackbourne stepped behind her and pulled at the ribbons, starting from the top, tightening the garment about her as he made his way down. Nearing the bottom grommets, he slowed to a stop.

She could feel his breath against the back of her neck as he leaned down, perhaps to take in her scent. She felt his desire surging to the surface, thrusting her body into some confusion.

Her mind prevailed. She stepped away and turned to face him. "Thank you, my lord. I can finish the rest."

Reaching behind herself, she managed to tie

the laces. When she met his gaze, his eyes seemed to burn with arousal. He looked every bit as ravenous as the wolves in the forest. He glanced away, agony twisting his countenance. She felt his conflict, the roar of desire coursing through his veins as he did his best to dam the tide.

"Shall I serve supper in the dining hall?" she asked, hoping to distract him.

"Do what you will," he grumbled, then brushed past her in his haste to leave.

She released the breath she had been holding. How was it she could now feel the torment inside of him, almost as if it were her own? What had he done to her? How often would she be faced with this?

His withdrawal had surprised her. He had not stopped himself before when he wanted to ravish her.

She dressed with half a mind, accidentally pricking herself several times as she pinned the frock.

After she had made supper and checked on Mr. Brooke, who was still asleep, she knocked upon Lord Blackbourne's door. "Your supper awaits, my lord."

She held her breath as he opened his door but

felt none of his earlier cravings.

Looking quite tired, he rubbed his eyes and grumbled, "I do not recall asking for supper."

"I asked if I should serve it in the dining hall."

"Ah. You did."

He followed her downstairs into the dining hall. It seemed a year had passed since she had served him and Miss Cameron. She wondered if her former mistress had received the letter she had drafted imploring the Camerons request her return from Lord Blackbourne.

He sat down and took in her change of attire. "The gown suits you, Miss Daliyah. Have you had supper?"

"Not yet, my lord."

"Then sit."

She blinked. Was he inviting her to sit at his table? When she did not move, he stood up and pulled the chair near his.

"Pray, sit," he said more gently.

Though she still preferred to keep her distance from the man, she sat down. He pushed his plate to her. Did he not like what she had prepared?

"You have more than earned your supper," he explained.

"But, my lord, I can see to my repast in the

kitchen," she protested. For the past several years, she had only ever dined at the servants' table. And servants did not have their meals until after the gentry had dined and their dishes cleared and rinsed.

"It would satisfy me to see you eat," Lord Blackbourne said.

"Are you not hungry, my lord?"

"I shall partake only after you have."

That left her little choice but to eat. He handed her his fork. Taking it, she took a bite of the potatoes. He sat back and watched.

"Tell me more of your family," he said.

"I have vague memories of my mother. When she passed, my father took me into the great house, but I spent most of my time with my grandmother."

"You said she was a healer of sorts?"

"Yes. Her village relied upon her before she was taken by a slave catcher and put aboard a ship to Barbados."

"And your grandfather?"

"I never met him. He was caught, too, but sold to a different plantation owner."

"Have the rolls and the butter," he directed.

"But these are the last of the rolls."

"Then enjoy them."

The finality of his tone made her think he would brook no protest. Had he decided to be nice to her to atone for his earlier treatment of her or because he was grateful for her care of his brother?

She ate without conversation for a spell, till, weary of the silence and a little unnerved by him watching her eat, she asked him, "Have you known Mr. Brooke since birth?"

"I had paid him no heed till the day I rescued the little fool from drowning. He followed me like a pup thereafter."

It pleased her to think of them as children and to know that Lord Blackbourne was capable of a good deed.

In search of more of the same, she said, "And you since became fast friends?"

"At first I merely tolerated his presence. I had no other siblings and was quite lonely at Castle Blackbourne, so it pleased me to have his company. I taught him how to hunt and ride. We generated our fair share of mischief."

"You enjoyed having a younger brother then."

"I knew not he was my brother till I was three and ten. His mother was a housemaid and often spoke of our likeness. I gave her comments little thought till, one day, I came upon my father tumbling her."

Daliyah wondered if the proverbial apple fell far from the tree. From the darkening of his tone at the mention of his father, she gathered his was not a simple affection.

"What happened to Mr. Brooke's mother?" she asked.

"When Mr. Brooke was twelve, she went to care for a sister in Liverpool. She contracted typhus and never returned."

"Mr. Brooke was but twelve?"

"I suppose I became at once a father and a brother to Addison. My father never acknowledged Addison as his son, though the likeness betwixt them is indisputable, while I bear a stronger resemblance to my mother."

"Is she the raven-haired beauty whose portrait hangs in the library in the west wing?"

"Yes. What were you doing in the library?"

"Looking for pen and paper."

"What for?"

"To write a letter."

He seemed to shift in discomfort and asked no further questions. "Finish the plate. You have thinned since you arrived."

"I could fix you a plate in the kitchen, my lord. Or do you prefer I cook something else?"

He waved a dismissive hand. "I've not the palate I once had."

Under his watchful eye, she continued to eat. His lordship had not touched any of the food, though his eyes glimmered with hunger.

He stood up abruptly. "After you are finished, be sure to look in on Addison."

He left her at the dining table alone, wondering what manner of hell she now occupied.

Chapter Twenty Four

Addison winced as Miss Daliyah applied a poultice to the gash on his leg.

"It would seem I owe my health to you, if not my life," he said as he drank in the sight of her loveliness, relieved and still astounded that she had but minor scrapes and bruises to account for her encounter with the wolves. She looked beyond comely in the dress Montague had given her. He was glad his brother had done at least one nice thing for her.

Miss Daliyah shook her head. "You would have mended."

"Perhaps. Perhaps not. Lord Bl—my brother had little faith in the doctor and credits you with my improvement."

"It is I who owe *you* my life," she replied as

she wrapped fresh linen over his wound. "Had I not crossed your path, I would have certainly met my end with the wolves."

And you would have had no cause to run into the forest if not for...

"They are wretched, cursed creatures," he said.

She paused after the word "cursed" but, finished with bandaging his leg, she attended to his shoulder next.

"I suppose we both owe our lives to Montague," he contemplated.

She was quiet and did not meet his gaze.

Addison swallowed with difficulty. "I am sorry you had to endure such a fright."

He was apologizing for more than the wolves, but did she know it?

"It is best to conserve your energy for healing," she replied.

Damnation. He would sooner have a morning star in his gut than the guilt that twisted there.

"Has Montague been good to you?" He needed to know.

He grimaced as she pressed the poultice over his wound. When she did not answer, he grasped her wrist, compelling her to look him in the eye.

"Has he?" he asked again.

At her silence, he felt the bile rise into his throat.

"Pray, tell me," he choked.

"He helped me chop the wood today," she answered.

Though he wanted nothing more than to hold her hand, Addison dropped her wrist so that she could continue working. "If it were not for the suffering he bears, he would be a different man."

She stared hard at him. "Is he even man?"

This time it was Addison who avoided her gaze.

"I saw his teeth lengthen and sharpen into fangs. He bit me. It felt as if he *drank* from me."

Addison wished she would press harder upon his wound. At that moment, he would welcome the pain.

"Tell me," she urged. "What is he?"

He continued to look away. She deserved to know the truth, yet no one apart from Montague and himself knew. Montague would be furious with him if he told Miss Daliyah. But how could he keep a secret she had already begun to discern?

"You know something but will not speak it?" she cried.

Reluctantly, he met her gaze. "He is part

man, part curse."

"What manner of curse?"

"A witch cursed him for refusing to marry her daughter, whom he had compromised. For his want of goodness and love, forever shall he be cursed to thirst for blood and lust for flesh. These appetites overcome him. They cannot be controlled and torture him from within."

She looked horrified. Her hands started to tremble. "He is compelled against his will to sink his teeth into me and ravish my body?"

"It is the work of the curse."

"And is it he who plants the sensations of desire in me?"

"It would seem the one act of grace the witch has bestowed to his victims that they may take some pleasure in their..."

Final breaths, he nearly finished, but had no wish to horrify Miss Daliyah further.

"You have been the only one to bring him some manner of satiation," he said. "I know not how or why you have succeeded where others have failed."

"There were others before me?" she asked.

"Alas."

Staring at the bed, she seemed to speak to herself. "It has always been him, and I had thought it all a dream." Looking up at him, she continued, "Have you known all this time of his curse?"

He felt frozen. The look of hurt in her eyes stung worse than salt to a fresh wound.

She backed away as if she could not bear to be near him.

"You should have left me to die," he murmured. "I will not ask your forgiveness for I deserve none of it. What I did is unpardonable."

She looked confused and desperate, like a mouse trapped in a corner. "I..."

Without finishing her sentence, she scurried from the room. Addison threw his head back and uttered a dozen oaths. If he had a knife upon him, he would have jabbed it into his thigh.

A few minutes later, Montague came into the room, asking, "What ails Miss Daliyah? She appeared quite flustered."

The muscles about Addison's neck and jaw tightened, but he said firmly, "I told her the truth."

Montague turned livid. "You... *what?*"

"She already suspected something amiss. You showed your fangs to her. She is no idiot."

"She once believed it all a fevered dream."

"Not anymore."

Montague cursed loudly. "She will have every reason to attempt to flee again now that you are returning to health. And I have a need to feed. I refrained myself earlier, but the hunger grows."

Misery washed over Addison as he watched Montague turn on his heels and leave. He could do nothing, Addison thought to himself. He attempted to raise himself from the bed, but his wounds screamed in protest.

I should have killed myself long ago. I had not the strength to kill Montague, but I could have taken my own life.

He wanted to do so now, but he could not leave Miss Daliyah to an uncertain fate. He roared in pain but pushed himself off the bed.

Chapter Twenty Five

Exhausted and intent upon seeing Mr. Brooke mended, Daliyah had not had the wherewithal to contemplate his culpability till now. Her head spun as she sat on her bed in the servants' quarters, far from both Mr. Brooke and Lord Montague. His lordship had the appearance of a man, but now she saw that her initial wariness of him was fully justified. Could he truly be cursed? She had never encountered, nor even heard of such a thing. Her grandmother, however, believed in witches.

She would not have left Mr. Brooke to die, but now that he was better, she would have less guilt in leaving him. Had he attempted to save her from the wolves so that his brother could continue to prey upon her? How could he betray her like this?

She wanted no more to do with either Mr. Brooke or Lord Blackbourne. She could not bear to spend the night in this castle of theirs. But it was evening. The wolves would be out. While she might have escaped unscathed the first time, she doubted she would be so lucky the second time. She would have to wait until the morning. Lord Montague seemed to rise late more often than not. Mr. Brooke would be in bed. If she were quiet, neither would be the wiser.

"What are you doing down here?"

She scurried to her feet at Lord Blackbourne's entry. Her pulse quickened. He stood at the threshold, blocking her egress. He narrowed his eyes, which seemed to her to glow with hunger.

"Hiding, perhaps?" he guessed, advancing a step. "You have a room upstairs."

"One I am not yet accustomed to," she said, taking her candle as if it might offer her some shield.

"You prefer the colder, barren accommodations here?"

"I need not finer quarters."

He kept stepping toward her. There would be

no escape, she knew. The man had bested several ferocious wolves.

Nay, he was not a man.

A pounding upon the door of the servants' entry startled both of them.

"What the devil be that?" his lordship demanded.

"I shall see to it," she replied, half expecting him to reach out and grab her by the waist as she hurried past him.

But he let her go.

She opened the door to find a man dressed in a worn coat and boots, his features pale and rough. Beside him stood Noah, the young man who had sold her the carving at the posting inn.

"'Tis you, miss," Noah remarked upon recognizing her.

The man grabbed Noah by the collar and shook him. "Hush! You're not to talk, eh?"

He turned to Daliyah and clearly knew not what to make of her. She was dressed in the garments of a lady but had not the complexion or grooming of one.

Lord Blackbourne came up behind her. "What is this? Who are you?"

Startled, the stranger doffed his hat. "Beggin' pardon, my lord. We lost our way in the forest.

My slave-boy here is frightened out of his wits, says there be wolves in these forests."

"Slave?" she echoed.

When she had first met Noah, he had said he and his grandfather were both free men.

"You've not come across the wolves?" his lordship asked.

"We heard them howling, like. While they scare me not, 'tis hard to find one's way in the dark."

"And you wish to seek refuge here for the night?"

"Aye, my lord, if it not be too terrible an imposition."

"You'll never find your way out of the forest at night, at least not alive. Your boy is correct, the wolves are fierce."

"You are most kind, my lord!"

"Are there but the two of you?" Lord Blackbourne inquired.

"And my wagon and horse."

"You may take the horse into the stables. I've not a full complement of servants at present. Miss Daliyah here can prepare rooms for you."

"I am most indebted, your lordship."

She bit her lip. A part of her wanted to warn them *not* to stay at Castle Blackbourne, but it was the lesser evil for now.

She hoped.

"What is your name, good sir?" Lord Blackbourne asked.

"Archibald Stone, at your service, my lord."

Mr. Stone turned to Noah and ordered him to see to the horse.

"What is happening?" came a voice from behind.

Turning around, Daliyah gasped to see Mr. Brooke leaning against the wall, his countenance twisted with pain.

"You fool!" Lord Blackbourne scolded. "What are you doing out of bed?"

Mr. Brooke looked to Daliyah. "I came to see that all was well with Miss Daliyah."

"That was most unnecessary. We have guests this evening, a Mr. Stone."

Mr. Stone nodded. Mr. Brooke appeared relieved.

"Come," Lord Blackbourne said, "I will assist you upstairs while Miss Daliyah takes care of our guests."

Once the brothers departed, Miss Daliyah asked if Mr. Stone wished for something to drink.

Mr. Stone leered at her. "Now what kind of

slave be you?"

She stiffened. "I am a servant, not a slave."

He smirked and looked about. "Where be the other servants?"

"There is only me at present."

He ogled her. "That so? A single maid living alone with two gentlemen?"

She went to boil water. "I can make tea for you both. There be some bread and cheese as well."

"There be any ale about here?"

Thinking Mr. Stone's manners would only worsen if inebriated, she replied, "I think not."

Mr. Stone grunted and sat himself down at the table. "Who was that man wrapped in bandages? Rather odd for him to be walking about in only his shirt."

"Mr. Brooke. He was viciously attacked by wolves. Noah was right to be afraid of them."

"You know my slave-boy, do you?"

"I met him at the posting inn once. He was working for himself."

Mr. Stone glowered at her. "He be my slave-boy now."

She decided she would sort out the circumstances with Noah.

"Now what manner of service be you providin'

the master of the house to have such a pretty dress?"

She flushed and went to grab bread and cheese, which she gave to the man in the hopes that he would be too busy to talk. She prepared the rooms that Emma and Jonathan had used. When she returned, she found Noah standing quietly while Mr. Stone took large mouthfuls of the bread. She made a plate for Noah.

"I didn't give leave that he can eat," Mr. Stone said. "Go to your room, boy."

"I will show him the way," she declared, taking the plate with her.

She showed Noah to the room adjoining the one she used to have and gave him the plate. "There be more if you are hungry still."

"Thank you, miss," Noah said as he sat down on the bed and ate eagerly.

"Who is this Mr. Stone? Where is your grandfather?" she asked, trying not to sound too worried.

"Mr. Stone says I be his runaway slave, which 'tisn't true. The magistrate told my grandfather to show proof that I be a freeman. We've no proof, never had any. The magistrate would believe only Mr. Stone."

Daliyah felt her heart break to hear this. "I

would something could be done."

"I worry for my grandfather. His sight be poor, and I have been his eyes these past years."

How she wished she could speak words of comfort, but what could she say? People like her, like Noah, were powerless, at the whim of the cruelty of others.

But she did have one thought. "If you could leave Mr. Stone and return to your grandfather, would you?"

"Of course, miss!"

"Then let us escape in the morning. If we leave early enough, they may not discover us missing for some time. I will ply Mr. Stone with ale that he might sleep late into the morning."

His eyes widened. "You mean to run away as well?"

"Yes."

"Are you certain no one will notice?"

"There is but his lordship and Mr. Brooke."

"There be no other servants? In such a big place as this?"

"There are none."

"My grandfather lives in a small hut near the edge of the forest. We will be safe there."

"It may be the first place they look if Mr. Stone knows of it, but yes, let us to try to reach your grandfather's place and decide from there. Be prepared to leave before the break of dawn."

Noah nodded. She sensed both nerves and excitement in him. Leaving him to finish his meal, she returned to Mr. Stone to tell him that she recalled now that there was ale to be had.

Chapter Twenty Six

Mr. Stone kept his eye upon her as he ate and drank. After providing him as much food and ale as she could, Daliyah went into the scullery to wash the dishes. She would stay the night in the servants' quarters to be near Noah. She would don her old garments so that she would attract less attention, perhaps even sleep in them so that she would waste no time in the morning. Before she went to bed, she would pack a light knapsack of refreshments. Aside from that, they would leave with only the clothes on their backs to make their travels light. Hopefully, it would be several hours before anyone discovered them missing.

"I think I be knowin' why there be no other

servants," Mr. Stone said from where he stood at the entry of the threshold.

She frowned as he walked closer.

"His lordship—or that other one—don't want folks knowin' they be tumblin' a wench of your kind," Mr. Stone continued.

Daliyah said nothing. A man like Mr. Stone deserved no response.

He stood beside her, near enough for her to smell his rancid breath and see the brown stains upon his teeth.

"Though I'd not blame them. You ain't too hard on the eyes for your sort."

She remained intent on drying the dishes. Her skin crawled beneath his gaze. If he touched her, she felt she would retch.

But she didn't when he grabbed her arm. "I be talking to you, wench! What? Think you be too good to look at the likes of me?"

She yanked her arm from his grasp and wondered if she ought to strike him with the pot that she held if he attempted to touch her again. That would surely only anger him. What would happen then?

Fortunately, the appearance of Lord Blackbourne saved her from having to decide what to do with the pot. His lordship's eyes narrowed at Mr. Stone.

"For what purpose do you speak with my maid?" Lord Blackbourne demanded.

Flustered, Mr. Stone began to stammer.

Seeing the anger blazing in Lord Blackbourne's gaze, Daliyah suddenly worried that he would throw Mr. Stone out. If that happened, Mr. Stone might take Noah with him.

"He was offering to assist with the dishes," she blurted.

Lord Blackbourne looked at her as if she were mad.

"Indeed," Mr. Stone seconded. "That be it."

"But I am nearly done and require no assistance," she added. "Thus, Mr. Stone can take his leave."

Lord Blackbourne glared at Mr. Stone till the man departed in some haste, without meeting his lordship's eyes.

"Why did you lie for him?" Lord Blackbourne asked.

"I wanted no trouble."

"You think a foul man like Mr. Stone might assist you somehow?"

In truth, she had not even considered such an opportunity, perhaps because she had not trusted Mr. Stone from the beginning.

"I know it now," she replied.

Lord Blackbourne walked over to her, standing mere inches away, making her heart hammer. "It is of no use to attempt to escape, Miss Daliyah. I will not let you go. Ever."

She thought to object. He had only till the end of her covenant. He did not own her. She was not his slave. But it mattered not. In the morning she would be gone.

"Did you come to seek my service, my lord?" she asked, her breath quivering slightly.

"I came to ensure that you had not forgotten about my brother while you tended to the guests. His right arm was left without bandages."

"Yes, my lord. I will tend to it immediately."

Scurrying past him, she went upstairs to Mr. Brooke. In her haste to leave him, she had indeed forgotten to wrap his right arm. She set her candle down beside his bed.

"I'm sorry," he whispered as she wound the linen around his arm. "Sorry for everything."

Not knowing what to respond, she remained silent.

"I would that it had been anyone but you, Miss Daliyah."

"How long has he borne this curse?" she asked, softening because he looked like he might cry.

"Two years."

"And you have known of it since the beginning?"

He nodded.

"How many women has he preyed upon?"

"It be not women only. Men have been his victims as well."

"Like Mr. Phillips?"

"Yes."

She started to tremble. "How many victims have there been?"

"In truth, I've lost count. He has tried his best—honest to God—to contain the curse. It eats him alive. He has, on dozens of occasions, tried to starve himself. He once asked me to kill him, but I was too much the coward to kill my only brother."

His pain cut into her. She would not have thought it possible to feel any sympathy for either Mr. Brooke or Lord Montague. They had conspired to harm and kill others. Yet, she saw the torture of their souls, a greater torment than that of the flesh.

"Our only hope has been to find the beauty who would lift the curse," Mr. Brooke continued.

"The beauty?"

"The witch who cursed Montague left us these words."

He quoted the curse to her.

"Is that why his lordship was interested in Miss Cameron?" Miss Daliyah inquired.

"Yes, but we know not *how* the beauty would break the curse. You have been the nearest relief for Montague. I know not how, but his appetites have never been satiated till he partook of your blood and flesh. You have survived where others have not. I think Heaven must have finally taken pity upon my brother and sent you as their angel."

"As a sacrificial lamb," she corrected. "Were I an angel, I could better help myself. While my lot in life is far more fortunate than others, I would hardly call my life enviable. To have my freedom snatched from me when it had been in reach. Now I am to belong to some manner of monster? What if he chooses not to set me free at the end of my indenture?"

She saw that her words pained him, as they should to anyone who had a conscience. He could not meet her gaze.

Finished with his bandages, she took her leave without further word. Despite her anger, which she believed righteous, she could not help but feel a sliver of sympathy for Mr. Brooke. It was plain that guilt, sorrow, and shame tore at him. If the tale he had told her be true, he had done nothing to cause Montague's curse, yet he bore it as much as his brother, mayhap more, for Mr. Brooke had more of a conscience and more decency.

However, tomorrow she would carve a new future for herself. She had endured enough for them. She owed them nothing. What amount Lord Blackbourne had paid to Miss Cameron for her indenture would hardly cause him to flinch.

Downstairs, she saw that Mr. Stone was clearly in his cups as he stumbled to his room. She stayed away from him. Though he would not have dared to attempt anything upon her while sober, especially after his encounter with Lord Blackbourne, his intoxicated state presented more unknowns. She did not relax till she heard his loud snoring.

While everyone slept, she packed what she thought could be carried. She had not had time to launder her garments, but donning unclean clothes was the least of her concerns. She considered staying up the whole night lest she wake too late in the morning, though doing so might weary her such that she could not make haste enough through the forest.

As she sat on her bed and vacillated about whether to close her eyes, she realized that not everyone was asleep. She heard footsteps in the corridor.

It was Lord Blackbourne.

Chapter Twenty Seven

"We should let her go."

Montague stared at Addison. His brother had finished partaking of the broth Miss Daliyah had made.

"And *why* would we do such a thing?" Montague asked.

"She has suffered enough," Addison answered as he shifted in his bed.

"Have *I* not suffered enough? Do *we* not deserve succor?"

Addison met his gaze. "This curse would not be upon us if you had agreed to marry the young woman you deflowered."

Montague's eyes widened. "Do you suggest I deserve to be punished as I have?"

"The curse was a consequence of your actions.

Miss Daliyah did nothing wrong. We need not add a third and innocent party to share in our torment."

Montague could hardly believe what he was hearing. "Do you know the number of victims I would have to feed upon and ravish to achieve the relief I get from her?"

"That is not her burden to bear."

"But the others who will certainly perish at my fangs deserve their fate? Miss Daliyah has the extraordinary ability to survive."

"And what if that does not last?" Addison replied in agitation.

Montague narrowed his eyes. "You've gone and fallen in love with the little trollop."

Addison looked away as if he would not demean to acknowledge Montague's comment. When he did look back, his eyes held anger. "She is no trollop—"

"Did she not willingly lift her skirts to you? And her virtue was compromised before she arrived. When I took her the first time, there was not a drop of blood—"

"She is no trollop!" Addison insisted. "She is as near an angel as can be had upon earth."

"She is as likely to be a witch as an angel. How else can we explain the effect she has upon me—and you? I would wager my life that you would not have recovered as quickly under the care of any ordinary doctor."

Addison seemed to consider what Montague said. "But if she were a witch with magical powers, how is it she cannot improve her lot in life? Instead, she has been damned as an indentured servant to that horrible Miss Cameron, and now to you. She was about to earn her freedom, an early end to her indenture, but you took that away from her."

Montague bristled. He did not want to have this conversation. "Have I not treated her better than Miss Cameron ever would? I gave Miss Daliyah a room no servant would ever have. I gave her fine clothes. I allowed her to sit at my dining table."

"You did? When?"

"Tonight. She hardly seems to have time to eat, and I wanted to ensure she did not faint from hunger."

Addison looked surprised and even curious.

"Once you are fully returned to health, she need not work at all if she desires," Montague proposed.

"She need only serve as your next meal and whore," Addison accused.

Montague scowled. "I did not choose this curse."

"Miss Daliyah desires her freedom above all. I think she would prefer it to all the riches you can offer her."

"Nonsense! Who would value freedom and poverty over bondage and comfort? And I could provide her all the comforts anyone would wish for. A woman like her could do no better, lest she became the mistress of a man with means."

Addison sighed. "I think it must be different for her, having lived in Barbados, surrounded by slavery and seeing the worst of that institution..."

"She will come to see the benefits of the life of comfort I am willing to offer her," Montague said, impatient to put an end to the discussion. "Mind you, I need provide her nothing more than bread and water. I could have her sleep in the dungeon, as I had thought to do—"

Addison straightened. "You thought to keep her in the dungeon?!"

"And more! Aye, I had considered much worse for her. I knew not whether you would live or die. You would not have been torn asunder by the wolves if not for her actions."

Addison looked too apoplectic to speak.

Montague felt his own wrath boil. This was the reaction he received for the love he bore his brother?

"Do you mean to take her tonight?" Addison asked through gritted teeth.

"I had thought to, but you are in luck. Mr. Stone and his slave are staying the night. For *your* sake, brother, I will choose one of our guests and not impose myself upon your beloved."

Turning on his heels, Montague stormed out. Of all people for Addison to fall in love with, why did it have to be Miss Daliyah?

Ready to tear down walls, he wanted to make his way straight to the servants' quarters. Addressing his appetites would calm the rage within.

But he went to his chambers to wait until everyone was asleep. After fuming for two hours, he went downstairs. Should he choose the boy or Mr. Stone? He decided on the boy, whose youthful vigor would provide a much better meal than Mr. Stone. The latter smelled sickly.

Montague stood in front of the room the young man occupied. At last, he would quench the thirst he had been holding back for the majority of the day.

A rustling sound stayed him from opening

the door.

"My lord?" Miss Daliyah whispered, stepping out into the corridor with her candle.

"Go back into your room," he commanded.

"Why?"

He looked at her sharply. "Because I said so."

"What is it you intend, my lord?"

"Are you ignoring my orders, Miss Daliyah?"

She pressed her lips together. Her brow furrowed with concern. "Noah is asleep."

"The better for him."

"Spare him, my lord."

After his vexing conversation with Addison, Montague was in no mood to have another. "Return to your room at once!"

He turned to face the door once more.

"Please, my lord!" she pleaded, grasping his arm.

He looked down at her hand. She dared to touch him in such a manner? Seeing his gaze, she dropped her hand.

"What of Mr. Stone?"

"You are partial to this Noah."

"He is but a boy," she said.

"He is near man enough."

"Have you no heart, my lord?"

He felt ready to explode. He snarled, "Have

you a wish to take his place, Miss Daliyah?"

She paused, then lifted her chin. "Yes."

He stared at her, sure that Eve herself could not have faced a greater temptation with the forbidden apple. His fangs lengthened as his mouth swam with salivation. His loins throbbed with desire.

But he had told Addison he would not take her tonight. He had two fish in a barrel that he could feed upon instead. It was a rare opportunity.

"You would do this for a stranger?" Montague asked.

"He has a grandfather who is blind, who depends upon him."

"Why should his troubles be yours?"

"Please, my lord, I am offering myself willingly to you."

He took in her perfect skin, soft and unblemished, and her lovely throat hiding behind a fichu—

He started. She was wearing her old garments, ones that he did not believe she had yet washed, when she ought to have been in nightclothes.

"Why are you dressed, Miss Daliyah?"

"I-I was working late and worried that I

would stain the fine frock you had given me," she replied.

"You overcame that concern earlier," he noted. "You washed dishes in that frock but have decided to change late into the night?"

She hesitated.

He grasped her by the throat, causing her to drop her candle. Her eyes widened in alarm.

"You meant to flee, didn't you?" he growled.

She clutched at his hand as she croaked, "My lord—"

"For this, I ought to make you watch me as I drain every last drop of blood from the young man you care so much for."

"If you spare him—I promise not to flee—"

"For certain, I shall see to it."

"I promise myself to you. Till the end of my indenture, I am yours."

"I need no such promises from you. I could have you chained in the bloody dungeon *and* partake of this Noah."

But Addison would never abide by such an action, though it were better if they did not have to mind her whereabouts every minute.

"Forever then," she blurted.

He stared at her. "You expect me to believe you?"

"If you will spare Noah and return him to his grandfather, if you promise to treat me as well as Mr. Brooke would—"

"Impossible. He is not cursed like me. I must have blood and flesh."

Her breath shook as she continued, "Apart from fulfilling the needs of the curse, could you be kind to me?"

"I was never the sort of person my brother is, even before the curse. He inherited all that was good in the Blackbourne blood."

"Could you try?"

He pulled her to him till her face was but an inch from his. "And for all this, you would place yourself in bondage to me?"

Her lashes fluttered. "Yes, my lord."

He withdrew and inhaled deeply. In truth, he had little to lose in agreeing to her proposition. There was Mister Stone upon whom he could satiate his appetite for the evening. After that, if she was true to her word, he could feast upon her for as long as he wished.

"Very well," he granted, "but to ensure you make no attempts to flee tonight, you will choose to spend the night in either the dungeon...or my bed."

Chapter Twenty Eight

Neither option appealed to Daliyah greatly, but, as a show of faith to Lord Blackbourne that she had resigned herself to be his, she answered, "Your bed, my lord."

Only then did he release his grip upon her throat. Her body trembled as she drew in much-needed air.

Taking her by the arm, he dragged her upstairs to install her in his chambers before he returned downstairs. Without her candle, she sat in the dark, too numb to find another candle to light. What if he did not spare Noah as he had promised? What if he changed his mind? Lord Blackbourne could do as he pleased, and she was powerless to stop him.

Except to deprive him of herself.

She thought of the men and women who had chosen death over slavery. She would, too, if he broke his end of the arrangement.

Had she spoken in haste? Should she not have promised herself to him? Perhaps she could have tried harder to persuade him?

No, he was unlikely to consider any argument she could make. She had felt his hunger. He would have a victim, and she could not have Noah's death upon her conscience.

If only his appetite had not reared its monstrous heads tonight, she might have had her freedom by day's end tomorrow. How quickly her fortune had turned! Now she had condemned herself to a life here at Castle Blackbourne.

After a period of time, she knew not how long, his lordship returned. She sensed much greater calm in him.

"Why do you sit in the dark?" he asked.

Why did he have no fire or candles lit in his chambers?

"I dropped my candle earlier," she said. "Is...is Noah still asleep?"

"He is."

"Can we return him to his grandfather tomorrow?"

"I can."

"May I accompany you?"

"Do you not trust me to deliver him as agreed?"

She knew not, but she preferred to be certain. "I met him at the posting inn, where he sold me a pendant. He was a freeman, he and his grandfather. Mr. Stone kidnapped him and claimed him for a slave."

"Well, he need worry no longer over Mr. Stone."

She was part relieved, part dismayed by the news. She shivered.

"You are cold," Lord Blackbourne remarked.

He went to the fireplace and started a flame. He cultivated it into a hearty fire.

"Thank you," she said, grateful for the gesture.

"The hour is late. You will want to sleep, but I'll not have you wearing your dirty garments into my bed."

Standing up, she began to unpin her dress while he sat in a chair and watched. She had kept the superior corset for it was too difficult to unlace herself, as well as the chemise and petticoats. She tried to pretend he did not rest his gaze upon every part of her body she exposed.

When she rubbed her arms to warm them, he rose from his chair and procured his banyan for her.

"I could sleep on the settee," she offered. *Or upon the floor.* She was not eager to share his bed.

He looked at her darkly. "Does my bed give you offense?"

She thought about offering to warm the bed, but it would only delay matters. Wordlessly, she made her way to his bed. The bedclothes were cool to the touch. She doubted she could truly fall asleep.

After she had settled into the bed, he turned around to face the fire. She expected him to come to bed at any moment, but he did not.

Deciding that if he intended to ravish her, she would sooner have it done than continue in her state of disquiet, she asked him, "Are you not coming to bed, my lord?"

"Since the curse, I have become somewhat nocturnal and prefer the night hours," he told her.

Like the wolves, she thought.

As if reading her mind, he said, "You need have no worries of me tonight. Go to sleep."

She curled her body beneath the bedclothes

and closed her eyes. Her heart heavy, she found it difficult to sleep. She kept wondering what she had committed herself to?

Lord Blackbourne was capable of kindness. She had seen enough evidence of it. He even had the capacity to love. She felt the strength of his affection for his brother. But he also had a weaker sense of morals, perhaps because of the curse, which she knew little of. Did the curse worsen with time? Mr. Brooke had implied it was improved with her.

Eventually, she fell into a shallow sleep and woke before the dawn. Prying her eyes open, she saw Lord Blackbourne seated, his gaze upon her. The fire still burned, suggesting he must have stoked it throughout the night.

"Did you not come into bed the whole night, my lord?" she asked.

"I did not trust myself to be so near temptation," he replied. "You slept little and fitfully."

"I should dress and see to Noah," she said.

He raised his brows. "It is early."

"We had both of us planned to run away this morning—at my suggestion. I could not abide by the thought of him taken away from his grandfather and enslaved by Mr. Stone." She paused. "Is Mr. Stone...?"

"I have disposed of Mr. Stone."

Daliyah looked down. Though she had not liked the man, she mourned the untimely manner of his end and even felt partially responsible.

"Must your prey always...is there no way for them to survive?" she asked.

"I would that they could, and have tried my best to curb my appetite. But the curse has always been a force greater than my will. I feed until there is naught left."

She looked upon him with unexpected pity. He had committed a wrong, yes, but his punishment was not in proportion to his sin.

Getting out of bed, she took her old garments to bring back downstairs. As she walked by Lord Blackbourne, he grabbed her arm.

"I may be more monster than man," he said, "but I would have you understand—this curse has changed me, you see."

Gazing into the depths of his eyes, she saw the emotions swirling within. "I see, my lord."

As if she had unsettled him, he abruptly dropped her arm.

"There are more frocks for you to choose from," he said, "and you will not stay another night in the servants' quarters. I want you nearer should I require you."

"Yes, my lord."

She continued on her way. After pinning on a new dress and grooming her hair, she went downstairs into the servants' quarters to find Noah pacing the corridor.

"Miss Daliyah!" he whispered. "I thought you had left without me!"

"I could do no such thing," she reassured. "Shall I make you breakfast?"

He looked at her in confusion. "Should we not make haste, before the others awake?"

"His lordship is awake."

His face fell.

"But not to worry," she added. "I told him how Mr. Stone abducted you and took you from your grandfather. He has agreed to return you."

Noah stared at her in disbelief. "But what of you?"

"Lord Blackbourne has more heart than I gave him credit for. In truth, I have not been long in his employment, and I miss my former mistress. But, for this act of kindness by Lord Blackbourne, I have decided to stay."

"Truly?"

She nodded and put on a large smile. "And

there is Mr. Brooke, whom you may have seen last night. He is a gentle soul. Come, I shall boil several eggs that you may take some to your grandfather."

"What of Mr. Stone?"

She looked to see that the door to the man's room was closed. "Let us hope the copious amount of ale from yester night will keep him asleep till noon."

"What if he comes after me when he discovers I am gone?"

"Perhaps Lord Blackbourne could have a word with the magistrate."

Noah remained nervous, but her words had mollified him enough to partake of breakfast. She gave him the knapsack she had prepared the night before. It included the money she had saved, which she would no longer need. Her hopes of an early freedom were no more.

Chapter Twenty Nine

Montague cursed as he struggled to tie his cravat in a pleasing manner. He would sooner not wear a neckcloth at all, but he had to as he was going into town. He would speak with the magistrate and require the man to consult with him on all matters of significance—such as the claiming of a blackamoor for a slave.

All this for Miss Daliyah.

He shook his head, still in disbelief that she would make such a sacrifice for the young man. If she were intelligent, however, she would see that she was better off here at Castle Blackbourne. While it may terrify her to be his prey, he would otherwise, unlike Miss Cameron, treat her with civility and fairness.

In truth, what was so terrible about submitting herself to him? Paid whores gave their bodies to strange men, some of them likely revolting. Miss Daliyah was fortunate in many respects. There was no reason for him to feel guilty about her lot in life. He rather regretted that he had not taken her last night. He had thought to only feed upon Mr. Stone, a barely satisfactory meal, and save his other appetite for Miss Daliyah, but he had told Addison he would not take her, and he wanted to show her that he could uphold his end of the arrangement.

He had attempted to sate his carnal hunger with Mr. Stone, but, in truth, he did not enjoy the act of buggery. He suspected that even if he had not found Mr. Stone as repulsive as he did, had he slept alongside Miss Daliyah, he would not have kept his hands to himself. He desired her...and not for the sake of the curse. This unsettled him.

After finishing a mediocre cravat, he tucked any superfluous fabric into his waistcoat and went to find Noah, to tell him to hitch Mr. Stone's horse to the wagon. Noah frequently glanced between him and Miss Daliyah as if worried some trickery was planned.

Montague rode his horse alongside them

while Miss Daliyah sat in the wagon with Noah, who did not seem to relax till they were in sight of the shanty where his grandfather lived. Noah immediately ran inside.

"Grandpapa, I have returned!"

Montague remained outside upon his horse while Miss Daliyah took in the knapsack and explained to the grandfather their good fortune.

"I must thank this glorious gentleman," the grandfather said.

Montague started. He had hoped to depart soon, but a few minutes later, assisted by Noah, the grandfather appeared. The old man barely had hair left upon his balding head. His eyes had the vacant stare of the blind.

"My lord, what we owe you would take a hundred years to repay," the old man said after Montague dismounted, "but whatever we can do, you need only ask."

"There is nothing to repay," Montague replied. "I am merely righting a wrong."

"Which you need not have done."

"You should direct your thanks to Miss Daliyah. It was she who pleaded your case before me."

At that, the old man showered Miss Daliyah with words of appreciation.

"Miss Daliyah, will you be taking the horse and wagon back to Mr. Stone?" Noah asked. "You must pull hard upon the reins, as the horse is aged and stubborn."

"That won't be necessary," Montague cut in. "The horse and wagon are yours to keep, a consequence for Mr. Stone so that he understands the extent of his wrongs."

Noah's eyes bulged. "The magistrate will think we stole the horse and wagon."

"I mean to speak with the magistrate about all of this."

He saw Miss Daliyah look at him in surprise. Then her eyes brightened, and it seemed her countenance glowed with gratitude.

Emboldened, Montague added, "I understand you sell carvings. Perhaps you could show me a few?"

Noah ran inside and emerged with several. Montague had no use for trinkets but offered to purchase all of them.

"Lord Blackbourne, you are beyond generous!" the grandfather cried. "How have we come to be so blessed by you?"

"Please credit Miss Daliyah," Montague reminded.

Eager to be on his way, Montague mounted

Aries and pulled up Miss Daliyah, settling her in front of him. The last time he had her between his arms upon Aries, the circumstances had been quite different. Now he liked riding with her.

"That were quite kind of you, my lord," she murmured after they had ridden in silence for several minutes.

Not wishing to discuss it, he said nothing. He looked over her hair. She had a great many curls, a few whom refused to be tamed. Overall, they looked rather unruly.

"You need a better headdress," he said. "We will stop by the milliner's shop."

"My lord, I've no money left."

"Did you truly think you were to pay?" he scolded. The foolish chit.

Once in town, he dismounted and assisted her from Aries. He ignored the stares they received.

Inside the milliner's shop, Miss Daliyah hung back, almost as if she were ashamed to be seen with him. But she more likely wanted to draw little attention to herself.

The milliner was an obsequious little man who greeted Montague with far too many words than necessary.

"I have little time and wish to purchase a

lady's bonnet," Montague interrupted him.

"Of course, my lord," said the milliner. "And what does the young lady like? We may be a small shop and far from London, but we do have several bonnets late from Paris."

Montague gestured for Miss Daliyah to choose one.

"This one will do," Miss Daliyah said, pointing to a simple straw bonnet, the plainest of all.

Displeased with the ugly bonnet, Montague walked over to the window display and eyed a pale blue silk bonnet with a pink bow and ribbons. Beside it was a straw hat with a large brim and decorated with feathers and silk flowers.

"These two will do," Montague pronounced.

While Miss Daliyah gasped, the milliner said, "It surprises me not at all that a fine gentleman such as yourself will have chosen the two best, most exquisite and most expensive—"

"Give the one to her now and wrap the other."

"Of course, my lord."

With some hesitation, Miss Daliyah put on the silk bonnet before a looking glass.

"Let's see the bonnet, child," Montague ordered, impatient with her fidgeting of the ribbons.

She turned around.

"It suits the young lady to perfection!" the milliner proclaimed.

Montague had to agree. She looked quite *adorable.*

"We have more of the silk bonnet but in different hues if she wishes to match her other dresses," the milliner continued.

"Perhaps a nightcap," Montague said. "And that one, with the ostrich plume."

"Certainly! And may I suggest this one with the lace trim and satin bow? I think the young lady will look charming with this one."

Miss Daliyah shook her head through it all.

"Let us see if what you say is true," Montague said.

"The one I have suits me," Miss Daliyah protested.

"The other might suit you better." She would not dare offer too much objection in public, would she?

She did not and dutifully removed the blue bonnet to put on the other.

"Fetching," Montague murmured. "Quite fetching."

When they were done, he had purchased half

a dozen to be delivered to Castle Blackbourne tomorrow.

Miss Daliyah was too flabbergasted to speak for most of the ride to the home of the magistrate, where she waited in the foyer while he spoke with the man in his office.

"Lord Blackbourne, 'tis an honor!" the portly man greeted, keenly peering at Montague through his spectacles as if he did not quite believe what he saw. "I thought perhaps you spent most of your time in London, as it has been so long since last we met. I remember your manservant, Mr. Brooke, saying you took ill for a long time, but I am pleased to see you appear in wonderful health now."

"Yes. I am feeling much better these days," replied Montague. "I came to see you about the matter of a man named Mr. Stone, who happened by Castle Blackbourne yester night. How is it you came to believe his word over that of the young man, Noah?"

"My lord?"

"What evidence did Mr. Stone present to claim ownership of Noah?"

"Er, evidence? He spoke quite persuasively."

Montague, quoting from Romans, said, "'By smooth talk and flattery, they deceive the minds of naive people.'"

The magistrate stammered and looked down. "I—he—he said the boy had run away from him. I thought it plausible."

"Is it not just as plausible that Noah was a free Negro, and Mr. Stone took advantage of the fact that the young man had no protector?"

"One hears more of runaways than free blackamoors, my lord."

"*I* have heard that magistrates are, more often than not, corrupt and prone to abusing their powers, but I am loathe to apply what I hear in general without taking into account the specifics of each case."

The magistrate hung his head.

"I took the liberty of restoring Noah's freedom," Montague continued, "and as recompense, I demanded Mr. Stone give up his horse and wagon to young Noah."

The magistrate looked dumbfounded. "Mr. Stone, he agreed to this?"

"He made no protest."

"That is amazing. You are quite the effective purveyor of justice, my lord."

"Henceforth, if you wish to consult with me on future cases, I am at your disposal. My father had you installed as magistrate, and I trust he had good reason for your appointment."

"I was honored then and am honored now to be of service to you, my lord. Pray consider me your humblest of servants."

After meeting with the magistrate, Daliyah asked to stop by the market. Having had enough of being in the sun, Montague told her to make it brief. She purchased ham and bread.

While headed back to the castle, they crossed paths with Mr. Thomson, who said he was about to pay Mr. Brooke a visit. Montague assured the doctor that future visits were unnecessary, as Mr. Brooke was recovering quite well. Mr. Thomson seemed quite surprised but also relieved that he no longer had to travel to Castle Blackbourne.

"You need not have purchased so many bonnets," Miss Daliyah said on their ride home.

He did not often ride at such a slow pace and preferred the gallop, but with Miss Daliyah with him, he enjoyed the more peaceful gait. A rare tranquility filled him as he rode through the forest with her.

"A proper woman would be grateful—nay, giddy—to receive so many," he replied. He did not reveal that he had never purchased a bonnet for a woman before.

"I am, my lord, grateful."

"You have an odd way of showing your appreciation."

"I cannot repay you—"

"They are gifts, you fool."

"Nevertheless, even as gifts, I feel indebted because of them."

"That is your cross to bear. You think I need to ply you with gifts when I can simply take what I want?"

He watched her bosom rise and fall with uneven breaths before taking in the curve of her cheek and the thickness of her lashes.

"Have the wolves always prowled these woods?" she asked.

"They have, though their numbers seemed to have grown of late. In the past, one rarely encountered more than one at a time."

"Are they cursed as well? I knew not wolves could be so large and vicious."

"I know not. Perhaps they are."

They rode in silence for a while longer before she said, "You were kind and generous to Noah, my lord."

"It were easier to leave the wagon and horse with them," he replied.

"You need not have purchased all his

carvings."

That was true. Seeing Noah's response to receiving the horse and wagon—and the light in Miss Daliyah's eyes—he had wanted to prolong their reactions.

"You can have the carvings," he said. *I have what I want between my arms.*

She was as relaxd in that moment as she had ever been near him. When they reached the castle, he wished the ride had lasted longer. After seeing to Aries and providing the horse food and water, they went into the castle—where they were greeted by Addison, holding a pistol.

He lifted it, aiming it at Montague.

Chapter Thirty

Let her go, Montague," Mr. Brooke said.
Daliyah looked at Lord Blackbourne, who blazed with anger. "Put that pistol down!"

But Mr. Brooke kept his pistol raised, though his hand shook. "We ought torment her no more."

"You damnable fool! She has agreed to stay."

Mr. Brooke appeared taken aback.

"In exchange, I spared Noah his life," Lord Blackbourne explained.

Mr. Brooke straightened. "It matters not. She deserves her freedom."

Daliyah felt Lord Blackbourne's wrath flare further. She also felt Mr. Brooke's conviction.

"Stand aside, Miss Daliyah," Mr. Brooke

ordered.

"'Tis true!" she exclaimed, not wanting to see another death. "I have agreed to this."

"An agreement under duress, no doubt, and to which you ought not have been placed."

"Mr. Brooke, please take yourself to bed. The course of action you are considering will not end well."

He stared at her. "It will end in your freedom. Take it now, whilst I still have the courage—"

"Courage?" scoffed Lord Blackbourne. "If you had had sufficient courage, you would have killed me long ago."

Mr. Brooke looked to his brother. "I would had I not loved you as much as I did! That would have made it easier!"

Lord Blackbourne strode over to him. "Then what stops you now? Have you not found a better love?"

Daliyah rushed to wedge herself between them. All she saw was death, regret, and misery—for both of them.

She turned to Mr. Brooke. "Pray, Mr. Brooke—"

"Addison. I should like to hear you speak my name once before—"

"Addison. All will be well. I am not afraid. I

was glad Lord Blackbourne agreed to the arrangement. He need not have. He could have done as he pleased and locked me in the dungeon. But he did none of this. You should have seen the kindness he showed Noah and his grandfather."

"Kindness?"

"And charity. He bought me this bonnet. Do you like it, Mr. Brooke—Addison?"

Her question befuddled him. He glanced at her headdress.

"I've never had such a pretty bonnet before," she continued.

His brow remained furrowed.

"And he bought me several more!" she said, sounding more like Miss Cameron than herself. She placed a hand over the hand holding the pistol and spoke softly. "Please say you like my bonnet, Addison."

"Of course," he replied.

"I assure you, there is nothing about you he would *not* like," Lord Blackbourne scowled.

Daliyah tried to will his lordship not to speak further or he would ruin the progress she had made with Mr. Brooke.

"Miss Daliyah, you are not safe here," Addison addressed her.

"I think I am," she told him. "It would appear that his lordship has not the same effect upon me as he has on others."

"How can you be certain of such an immunity? What if it wears off? What if his hunger grows?"

"Miss Daliyah appears blessed with healing properties," Lord Blackbourne said. "You have witnessed firsthand her abilities."

"But your appetites persist."

"You would rather I return to hunting prey after prey? Do you wish for more deaths to be notched upon our conscience?"

Daliyah stepped closer to Mr. Brooke, drawing his attention. "I wish to stay, Mr. Brooke."

He searched the depths of her eyes as if to ascertain whether or not she spoke sincerely.

"Addison," he said.

"Addison," she repeated gently and warmly.

His hold on the gun relaxd, and she took it from him. Taking the pistol from her, Lord Blackbourne uncocked it.

"You are weak still," she said to Mr. Brooke, noting that the incident seemed to have drained him. "Let me assist you back to your chambers."

Holding him by the arm, she helped him limp

back up the stairs. Sensing Lord Blackbourne seething still, she did not look back.

"You should have allowed me the chance to set you free," Mr. Brooke murmured after she had settled him into his bed.

"And have tragedy come betwixt you and your brother?" she replied as she checked his bandages. "I want no more deaths upon my conscience."

"It is not a sacrifice you need make. This is none of your doing."

"Perhaps it is my destiny."

His countenance darkening, he scowled, "It is a damnably foul fate for a soul as brave and good as yours."

"There are those braver and better than I, whose lives are far worse."

He grabbed her hand. "If my brother—if you should find your situation worse, or you have a change of heart, you have but to inform me."

Dear Mr. Brooke, she thought to herself. She pressed his hand.

"You are too forgiving, Miss Daliyah."

"Perhaps, but life is harder without forgiveness."

He looked at her as if in awe before expanding his gaze to take in all of her. "No one could look more fetching in that bonnet."

"Would you believe your brother chose it for me?"

At that, Mr. Brooke frowned. "He ought to do more than buy bonnets for you in return for what you are sacrificing. I hope he did not coerce you?"

"I feel as if I have one death upon my conscience already."

"Who?"

"Mr. Stone. I could not have more."

"Think no more on it. It will only make you more miserable. I know it."

"Let me prepare a proper repast for you if you feel you can have more than the tea and broth I have made thus far."

"I owe my health to you. Would you eat with me?"

"I will join you after I have prepared a meal for Lord Blackbourne as well. He partook of no breakfast this morning."

"His only appetite is for blood and flesh."

She considered all the times Lord Blackbourne had sat down to dine. Perhaps he had taken a bite or two, but it was true that he did not eat.

"He drank quite a bit the other night," she recalled.

Mr. Brooke sighed. "He drank himself into several stupors the first months of the curse, but the intoxication succeeded in naught but giving him wretched headaches and bouts of retching. It did nothing to soothe his hunger and cravings."

Daliyah tried to imagine the pain Lord Blackbourne must have suffered. She had an inkling of his thirst. To endure that every day for as long as he had was truly awful.

"I take it you've not been able to find the witch that cursed your brother?" Daliyah asked.

"Alas, we have searched every corner of England and sent men to the Continent and as far as the colonies in America. It is as if she existed only to place her curse upon Montague."

He closed his eyes. Leaving him to rest, she took her leave. She paused at the top of the stairs. To her left was the corridor that led to Lord Blackbourne's chambers. He was in there. She knew without seeing or hearing evidence of this.

She remembered her first night at Castle Blackbourne and how she had sensed his presence in the shadows. Even with Mr. Brooke's kindness, she had hoped they could leave Blackbourne with all speed, not knowing that she might be spending the rest of her days here.

Chapter Thirty One

Would Addison truly have shot him? Montague wondered as he placed the pistol in a drawer and slammed it shut. All to protect Miss Daliyah? He would choose this woman over his brother, with whom he had spent his whole lifetime?

Perhaps Miss Daliyah had cast a spell of her own upon Addison. She had qualities suggesting she might have more in common with witches than with men. For certain no ordinary human could have such goodness and purity of heart as she appeared to possess.

No one save Addison, that is.

Montague threw himself onto a sofa in his chambers. He supposed his brother and Miss Daliyah were suited to each other. Perhaps they shared a bond reserved only for those with the most benevolent of spirits.

Yet they were fools, both of them. Addison had the chance to leave his brother to his fate. Instead, the dolt chose to remain and suffer alongside him. Miss Daliyah could have left Noah to *his* fate. Instead, she sacrificed her chances at freedom. It remained to be seen if she would keep her word, but Montague would see to it that she did.

But what if she and Addison decided to collaborate against him?

"How ironic," Montague muttered.

When it became clear that he could not stop his appetites, he had wanted only death. But he had not the fortitude to blow out his own brains and had asked Addison to do it. Addison, alas, weakened by his love, could not pull the trigger either.

Till now. Now that a possible cure existed, Addison found the courage!

It were possible that Addison would not have shot him still, but his brother had looked fairly determined. If Miss Daliyah had not intervened, Montague would have stepped in front of the pistol and dared Addison to shoot.

Why had Miss Daliyah intervened? If

Addison had shot him, she would have her freedom. Was it out of love for Addison that she chose to remain?

If he were less selfish, Montague would release the two lovebirds and urge them to go live their lives free of the burdens of the curse.

But he was not so selfless.

He had no wish to suffer his curse alone, without his brother. And though Miss Daliyah had not been long with them, he liked having her presence in the castle, not merely as a source of sustenance and flesh to ravish. His mouth watered as he recalled how she tasted. His groin warmed as he relived how glorious she felt when she spent. It almost eclipsed his own climaxs.

A part of him wanted to go find her now. Would Addison attempt to stop him? How would it feel for Addison to kill his own brother?

"My lord?" Miss Daliyah called after she had knocked without answer.

Montague remained where he was. If he opened the door, he would want to pull her into his room.

She knocked again. He heard her balancing dishware on a tray. When still he did not respond, he heard her walking away.

He closed his eyes. How easy his life had been

before the curse! While Miss Daliyah seemed to provide him relief, she had complicated his life. Were he and Addison better without her?

The question remained unanswered as he drifted off to sleep.

He woke just after twilight. His thoughts immediately went to what had happened with Addison. Getting up, he retrieved the pistol from the drawer and went to his brother's chambers.

Standing at the threshold, he heard Addison, his voice full of cheer, saying, "You've a natural ability at *vingt-et-un*, Miss Daliyah!"

"It seems more a game of luck," she replied.

"One can also make their own luck, as you have."

Feeling a touch envious of the easy rapport betwixt the two, he cut into their card game. He noticed Miss Daliyah sat upon Addison's bed and doubted she would have taken to *his* bed had he not forced her to.

"I will have a word with my brother," he told Miss Daliyah.

"Would you believe she won four of six hands in her first attempt at *vingt-et-un*?" Addison asked. His eyes always seemed to glimmer when he looked upon her.

"At first glance, it seems impressive,"

Montague allowed, "but you were never that difficult to best at cards."

"I won a decent proportion."

"When I let you."

He waited as Miss Daliyah collected the cards, the air in the room now somber.

"Would my lord care for supper?" she asked before passing him.

"No."

When he said no more, she took her leave. Montague closed the door behind her. Turning to face Addison, he tossed the pistol onto the bed. It landed near his brother's hand.

"I am returning it to you," he explained, "for when you have finally roused enough courage to shoot me."

Addison looked down at the firearm.

Guessing his brother's thoughts, Montague continued, "You remember I gifted that pistol to you on your fourteenth birthday."

"I remember," Addison said quietly.

"Would it not be fitting for me to die by the very weapon I procured for you?"

"Do you still wish for me to end the curse?"

"Does it matter what I wish?" Montague retorted.

"Of course."

"It did not matter to you when you had intended to shoot me earlier. Is it not more important to you to be Miss Daliyah's hero?"

Addison pressed his lips into a firm line. "She deserves a better fate than the one we are imposing upon her."

"Do we not all? For certain, *you* deserve better. And while I am far less saintly than the two of you, do I deserve the depths of this curse? Do those whose lives I have drained?"

"Did she truly agree to stay here of her own accord, knowing what she would be subjected to?"

Montague scowled. "What does it matter? *I* require her here."

Addison responded with equal vexation. "Perhaps the curse does suit you if you are incapable of caring for anyone but yourself."

"Miss Daliyah is an indentured servant. A slight of hand by providence and she would have been a *slave.* Her prospects in life were never very good."

"That is no excuse. Slavery is a horrid institution and indentured servitude little different."

"Since when were you an abolitionist and Jacobin? I know. Since you set eyes upon Miss

Daliyah!"

"I allow that since seeing her plight firsthand and having heard her descriptions of Barbados, I have been better acquainted with the evils of slavery."

"Do you see me forcing her to labor in some bloody field? Where else would she be wearing the garments of a noblewoman and be gifted a half dozen bonnets in one day?"

"A hundred bonnets would be no substitute for her freedom!"

"Freedom for what? To live in abject poverty?"

Addison made no response. His jaw clenched, he did not look at Montague.

"You can treat her however you wish," Montague said. "She need not lift a finger once you are returned to health. Have her live like a bloody princess here at Castle Blackbourne if that is what you desire. I have but one need of her, and I will satisfy that need tonight."

Chapter Thirty Two

Addison frowned at his brother's declaration. "Did you not feed upon Mr. Stone but yesterday?"

"I did not satiate the *other* appetite," Montague replied.

"Why not?"

"Why bugger a lowly cretin when I can have Miss Daliyah?"

Addison stared at Montague. *Damn you.*

Montague waited in silence, as if expecting to provoke a reaction from his brother. Addison glanced at the pistol near his hand.

"I took the shot out," Montague told him, "but I can put it back in."

"I'll do it myself," Addison grumbled. "I will not have Miss Daliyah's death upon my hands.

If your appetites overcome you…"

"By all means," his brother all but dared.

Addison released a large breath. Would he truly choose Miss Daliyah's life over his brother's? Perhaps it would be different if Montague had a life worth living. Death would be a savior.

The affection I bear for Miss Daliyah may give me the strength I have wanted for so long to put my brother out of his misery.

Montague's countenance remained dark and stoic. Addison wondered if Montague worried that he loved Miss Daliyah more than his own brother? He wanted to assure Montague that he did not love his brother less, but he doubted he wanted to hear it or would believe it.

"I wish to be there when you take her," Addison said, "that I may keep watch on your appetites."

Montague smirked. "Merely to watch?"

Addison colored.

"I have no desire to destroy my only source of succor," Montague informed him, "but you are welcome to protect her."

Montague opened the door just as Miss Daliyah appeared holding a tray with soup, ham, and bread. Their gazes briefly met. Addison saw the flare of lust in Montague's eyes.

What he saw in Miss Daliyah's eyes was not the alarm he had expected.

"My lord," she greeted in a soft voice.

Montague walked past her without saying a word.

Miss Daliyah was quiet in thought before saying, "Your supper, Mr. Brooke."

Addison got out of bed, grunting when his body protested. She set the tray on a table in the sitting area and rushed to his side.

"You need not," he told her. "I feel stronger by the minute. But I will have you dine with me, if you would."

She joined him at the table. "The ham and bread were purchased this morning."

"My brother took you to the market?" he asked as he partook of the soup she set before him.

"Is it odd that he did?"

"He tolerates the sunlight better after he has fed. I remember a time when he had gone days without feeding. He had hoped a good gallop on Aries would settle his appetites, but after a few minutes in the sun, he could not bear it."

"Has he tried feeding upon the blood of animals?"

"Countless times. Once, I came into the barn to find it covered in blood, every pig slaughtered, even the piglets. Alas, they do little to satisfy him."

"What a horrid witch who cast the curse! She has condemned not just your brother but many innocent lives."

"And while I allow that my brother has his faults, his sin was not so great that he deserved this."

"You, too, have shouldered this curse."

"And you."

Quiet descended between them till he said, "Pray, eat, Miss Daliyah. You will need your strength."

She raised her brows.

He cleared his throat and sighed. "My brother intends..." How should he say it? What words to choose?

"I know," she said.

He wondered if perhaps she had overheard them speaking. "You know?"

"I felt it. His desire."

"I will be present. To ensure you come to no harm. Rather, I should say..." He balled his hand into a fist.

She placed her hand over his. "I think all will

be well. I have survived this several times before."

"The victim should not be the one offering comfort," he said bitterly.

"It does not hurt—much. The bite is the worst. After that, it is as if a venom fills my veins, and my body is overcome with the same appetite as his."

"Is this curse not most dastardly? To make the victim a party to their own demise?"

"But I would rather perish in the grips of desire than fear."

He opened his fist to grip her hand, then exhaled a shaky breath. "I cannot commend your courage enough, Miss Daliyah. After all the wrong we have done you, will do—"

"Let us not dwell on that. There is much we can yet be grateful for."

Addison shook his head. Would Miss Daliyah never cease to amaze him with her graciousness? Neither he nor Montague deserved it.

Mere nights ago, he and Miss Daliyah had shared a bed, their bodies connected as one. It had been the most beautiful night he could remember. Though he knew it to be a stolen moment and such bliss could not be sustained, he had dared hope for more. She had felt right in his arms.

All that was now lost.

Instead, he had to witness his brother take what Miss Daliyah had freely given to *him.*

For Miss Daliyah's sake, he lamented no more. He insisted on assisting her with the dishes, but she refused him, arguing that a fast recovery would prove more beneficial to her in the long term. When she helped him change into a fresh shirt, it took all of him not to sweep her into his aching arms when her fingers brushed against his skin. It seemed her breath grew uneven, and her gaze seemed to linger upon his body. Could it be that he did not repulse her? He thought for certain his mangled flesh would horrify her.

An hour or so after she had left him, Montague appeared in his chambers. "Is Miss Daliyah done with her chores?"

"I think not. There is too much to be done for one person," Addison said.

"We can discuss it on the morrow. For tonight, when she is done, you will bring her to me."

Chapter Thirty Three

Montague could have easily fetched Miss Daliyah himself, but a part of him wanted to put his brother in his place. Returning to his chambers, he waited for them with only the fire from the hearth providing light. It would seem contrary of him to lament how the curse had also ensnared Addison, yet be no less angry at his brother for drawing his gun on him.

He rose when they entered. Miss Daliyah was in full dress. Addison stood behind her. He had his pistol with him

She bobbed a curtsy. "My lord."

"Come here," he commanded of her.

She approached him without word. His gaze took her in from head to toe. The frock fit her well and displayed a lovely cleavage above the square neckline.

"We ought to have gotten you a new mobcap," he said of the slightly discolored headdress. "Though a servant's cap does not pair well with your new gowns. Remove it."

She did as told.

He debated when to sink his fangs into her. A part of him wanted to know how she would truly react, unadulterated by his venom. Was there any part of her that would welcome his touch? Or would she want to resist him?

She gasped when he cupped her chin.

"Fear not, my dear," he assured. "I will be gentle."

"He will indeed," seconded Addison.

Suppressing a scowl, Montague kept his attention upon Miss Daliyah. "These garments are quite cumbersome. Let us discard them."

One by one, she removed her pins and peeled the top of the frock from her shoulders. The gazes of both men lingered upon her bare arms. Next, she unpinned the skirt of her frock. It slid to the floor with a satisfying rustle. After untying her petticoats, she stood in only her stockings, chemise, and corset.

Montague salivated. He could see the flame

of arousal in Addison's eyes, too.

Montague turned her around to face Addison so that he could unlace her corset. He did so slowly, purposefully, drawing out Addison's discomfort to prove he could and would dictate all that transpired in his castle. Tossing aside the corset, he embraced her from behind, pressing his erection into her backside. She drew in a sharp breath. Addison shifted and averted his gaze. Montague smiled to himself as he groped a breast through her chemise. His other hand cupped her mons.

"How delicious you smell and feel, my dear," he murmured into her hair as he breathed her scent in deeply. His groin throbbed.

Kneading the orb he held in one hand, he rubbed her between the thighs with the other. She whimpered. Was that dampness he felt?

"When do you intend to bite her?" asked Addison.

I may not need to, Montague considered, observing Miss Daliyah's uneven breaths. She shivered, but not in fear.

"Perhaps she would rather I not," he said.

She and Addison looked at each other. The latter furrowed his brow, likely weighing the difficulties of the options. Biting her would spare her the horror of being ravished against her will, but it would also give Montague a taste of her blood, of which he might want more.

He rubbed her quim through the fabric. It was definitely wetness his fingers felt between her legs.

Nonetheless, he gave her a choice. "Do you wish for my fangs?"

She hesitated. "Yes, my lord."

Her answer disappointed him. He would have relished showing Addison that she desired him of her own accord. But for Addison to watch his beloved in the arms of another man was likely torture enough.

Miss Daliyah held the curls off her neck. Lowering his head, Montague sank into her. A bonfire of arousal ignited in his groin. Though Mr. Stone had diminished Montague's thirst for blood, Miss Daliyah tasted so heavenly, he was tempted to drink past his fill.

"Enough!" Addison ordered.

Montague withdrew his fangs and tightened his grip upon Miss Daliyah. His hands would feast upon her body instead. She started to moan and writhe. Montague saw the tenting of Addison's breeches at his crotch.

His own cock demanded to be fed, but he was

more intrigued by Miss Daliyah's motions at the moment. She placed her hands over his, making him squeeze her breast and press harder against her quim. Her head fell back against his chest as she ground herself into his hands whilst groaning and panting. His cock seemed to tingle with her pleasure. He withheld his own need in favor of hers.

With their own breaths uneven, the brothers watched her as she edged closer and closer to the ultimate carnal rapture. With a cry, her body shaking, she spent in Montague's embrace. He felt as if her bliss overflowed from her body into his. But his cock raged for its own climax.

Picking her up in his arms, he dropped her onto his bed, then ripped her chemise down the middle. He drank in the sight of her naked body, from the swell of her breasts to the patch of hair at her mound. She was lovelier than the most erotic of paintings.

He licked the blood from her neck, then kissed his way down to her bosom. She cried softly when he took a nipple into his mouth and sucked. Threading her fingers through his hair, she gripped him tightly as he suckled the other breast. He kissed his way down to her navel before settling himself between her thighs, heavy with the scent of her desire. He breathed her in and noted her copious amounts of moisture.

"What are you waiting for?" Addison grumbled, clearly wanting this all to be over.

Straightening, Montague began divesting himself of his clothing. Meanwhile, Miss Daliyah caressed herself. It was a sight to see.

"My God," Addison whispered.

Standing naked, Montague stroked his hardened shaft as he watched Miss Daliyah squirm upon his bed.

"Take me, my lord."

He glanced toward Addison and smirked. Looking back at her, he bid, "Say again what it is you wish."

"I wish you to take me, my lord. Ravish me."

Her words were music to his ears. Needing no further encouragement, he pulled her to the edge of the bed where he stood and speared himself into her wet heat. She cried out in surprise and possibly some pain. He had not intended to shove himself so hard and deep, but his ardor had grown too powerful to contain.

Holding onto her legs, he thrust into her. Her grunts and gasps, the smacking of their flesh, were sounds more melodious than the finest of operas. Every thrust stroked the tension of pleasure and need. He could not bury himself far enough in her.

He quickened his pace and hurled himself into blinding euphoria. He roared his release as he rammed his cock in fury. A violent paroxysm shook and stretched his body. He had not thought his body capable of such ecstasy. As he pumped the last of his seed into her cunnie, his heart continued to beat as if it wanted to escape its walls.

She bucked her hips, wanting more, but he was too spent. Looking over at his brother, whose countenance could easily be a mix of disgust and desire, he decided to grant Addison what he must desire most at the moment.

Withdrawing from Miss Daliyah, he said to Addison, "Have at her."

Chapter Thirty Four

As Daliyah lay upon the bed, her body warm with desire, she heard Mr. Brooke echo his brother's words in anger.

"'Have at her?' She is no slice of beefsteak you have deigned to share."

"She does not appear offended," Lord Blackbourne said as he sat down beside her.

"That is because you have poisoned her with arousal. I doubt she has paid any attention to what you have said."

"A state which you can now take advantage of—as you had before, lest you think yourself too honorable."

They both looked to her, watching as she fondled the nub of pleasure between her legs and groped a breast. Mr. Brooke was not wholly correct. While she did feel desire coursing strongly through her, she had caught every word of theirs, every exchanged glance between the brothers. She saw the pained physiognomy of Mr. Brooke and the curl of smugness upon Lord Blackbourne's lips.

"She can be quite the charming little slut, eh?" Lord Blackbourne commented as he brushed his thumb over her parted lips. He pressed the digit into her mouth. She closed her lips about him and sucked.

"Only because you have made her one," Mr. Brooke retorted.

"And you played no part? She was under no false pretenses when she lifted her skirts beneath *you*."

Mr. Brooke stepped toward Lord Blackbourne. Fearing they would come to fisticuffs, she sat up, ready to interpose herself between them. "Pray, Mr. Brooke—Addison, will you not take me, too?"

He did not look at her.

"Do you find me too whorish to bed now?" she asked.

Turning to her, he looked horrified at the thought. "Miss Daliyah—"

"Daliyah," she corrected. "If you would have

me call you Addison."

"I could not."

"Why not?"

"It hardly seems right."

She pursed her lips together before saying, "But I desire it."

"Do you?"

Sliding from the bed to the floor, she knelt before him and gazed at his crotch. She started to undo the buttons of his fall.

"Miss Daliyah!" he said, grasping a hand with his.

"Pray, let me."

With her free hand, she rubbed his hardened member through his breeches. He groaned. She managed to unbutton his fall with the one hand. Giving in, he released her other hand. She pulled out his cock, wrapping her fingers about the shaft. His chest heaved with every breath but stopped when she lightly kissed the top of his member.

Curious, she covered his tip and flare with her mouth, tasting of him, feeling him throb inside her orifice.

"Damn me," Lord Blackbourne uttered.

Sensing Addison's wonder and arousal, she decided to take more of his length into her mouth.

"Miss Daliyah…" he murmured.

But she took away the last of his resistance when she sank even farther down his cock. She pulled her mouth up, felt him shiver, then decided to go back down.

"My God!" he whispered.

Emboldened, she repeated this motion several times, till her own desire cried for attention. She stood, then pulled Mr. Brooke by his shirt onto the bed and urged him onto this back. After pushing aside his shirt, she straddled him and sank herself onto his erection. He throbbed inside her.

Relishing the fullness, the hardness, she ground her body atop his. Grunting, he grabbed her by the hips and, despite his injured arms, assisted her motions. While pumping her thighs, she fondled both her breasts, seeking to send them both into ecstasy. Focused on securing a second helping of rapture, she vaguely noticed Lord Blackbourne stroking his cock to hardness as he watched.

She came undone when Addison pressed a thumb to the nub of pleasure. As she shook atop him, he bucked his hips hard and fast till he spent with a long, loud grunt.

After bliss had washed away the tension in their bodies, she slid off him to lay betwixt him and Lord Blackbourne. Laying on her side, facing Addison, she sighed with contentment. Behind her, Lord Blackbourne reached for her, pressing his member, hardened again, against her rump. His hand nestled between her thighs, where his fingers found her slick with moisture. He slid his other hand beneath her and cupped a breast.

Her arousal had settled to a simmer but found new life in his caresses, relishing how his digits grazed against the still swollen bud between her folds. She found herself pressing back against him. He angled his cock to fit between her legs, found her wet opening, and slid inside. She savored the sensation of the novel position of penetration. Her body pulsed about his shaft.

"'Sblood," he said. "Do you know how delightful your cunnie is?"

Holding her, he started to roll his hips, seeking her depths with his shaft. She circled her forefinger and middle finger over her clitoris while he thrust. His breath was hot upon her neck, his hand firm upon her breast.

With a new series of grunts and groans, she

impaled herself upon him till his motions increased in force and she could no longer match his rhythm. Entwined, they worked each other toward a mutual finish. She spent first, spasming hard enough that she nearly came off him. He grabbed her hips and bucked himself hard and fast to his release. He stabbed himself into her as he spent with a growl that could have been mistaken for pain instead of pleasure.

She felt him inside her, throbbing, before he withdrew several minutes later. He rolled onto his back. Closing her eyes, she allowed herself to drift to sleep betwixt the two men.

When she awoke, she found herself curled into Addison, his arm about her protectively. Lord Blackbourne was nowhere to be found. Her thighs were moist with the mettle that had seeped from her during the night.

It had not been a dream. She had allowed both men between her legs.

"You're blushing," Addison said gently.

She colored more. "Was I too harsh with you last night?"

"You were...magnificent, Daliyah." At her surprise, he added, "You allowed I could address you as such."

"Yes, I remember."

She felt the bite marks on her neck. When Lord Blackbourne had asked if she wanted his fangs, a part of her had thought it unnecessary. Her head spun that she could be so at ease with her present situation. Never would she thought herself capable of taking two men to bed at once!

"I should dress and see to breakfast," she said.

But Addison pulled her back to him with surprising strength.

"Your arm is much better," she noted.

"Indeed, I feel even more healed in one night than ever before. It is a near miracle."

Their gazes locked.

"I meant what I said," he continued. "Montague may be my brother, but I'll not see you harmed."

She believed him, but she also suspected that killing his brother would kill *him*.

"It will not come to that," she assured him. "The worst is behind us."

Softly, he cupped the side of her face. "You are...kind...to think so."

"And naive?" she guessed of what he had left unsaid.

"When you've lived with the curse as long as we have, hope appears an illusion. The nightmare is the reality."

She saw the years of pain in his eyes and was impressed that it had not broken all of his spirit, that there could still be generosity and compassion in him, rather than the bitterness present in Lord Blackbourne.

Chapter Thirty Five

Montague rarely slept at night and preferred to nap during the day. This night, however, he had fallen asleep in his own bed for several hours while it was still dark. Sometime in the night, Miss Daliyah had nestled toward Addison, who, in turn, had wrapped an arm about her.

Of course she had chosen Addison, Montague thought to himself as he observed the two in peaceful slumber together. Addison was the safe choice, the kinder choice. Yet, Montague wondered, had he not been cursed, would Miss Daliyah have ever considered him over Addison?

Every other woman would have, surely. A nobleman, he had wealth and breeding. That alone would have thrilled most women. The addition of his striking features, intelligence, and command surely made him among the most desirable of men. Addison, born a bastard, had naught but his handsome features, rugged figure, and pleasing disposition.

Addison and Miss Daliyah suited each other, however, both in standing and temperament. Despite their lot in life, they found things to be grateful for, whereas he, the Earl of Blackbourne, felt he had nothing to be grateful for. And despite all his outward trappings, he felt as if Miss Daliyah was *too good* for him.

While he had eschewed the church as a young man save for the requisite few times he had to attend, and twice when he thought doing so could help with his curse, he knew enough about morality to know that Miss Daliyah had a heart more pure than his. That he could take advantage of her for his own survival was not his fault. God was as much to blame as anyone.

Leaving Miss Daliyah and Addison, Montague rose. He donned a shirt and banyan and made his way downstairs to sit in solitude in the music room. The sun had yet to rise, but the shade of black outside had lightened.

A woman like Miss Cameron was a better fit for him, though he knew not her family and suspected them to be of the bourgeoisie. He could certainly aspire to a woman of higher standing, the daughter of a duke even. However, he had no interest in taking a wife. He only needed one to bear his successor.

He had told Miss Cameron that he would join her in London, but now he doubted he would. He found her company tedious. Her beauty stirred nothing in him.

Instead, his mind wandered back to his congress with Miss Daliyah. Her body, supple and shapely, called to all that was primal within him. And when he was buried inside her, he could think of and feel nothing else but her. When she spent, her cunnie pressing or fluttering against his cock, it was beyond marvelous. He wanted to make her spend over and over again.

He rather missed the time he'd had her to himself, without Addison. But Miss Daliyah likely found Addison's presence reassuring, and Montague would rather she be comforted than not.

When it was bright enough outside, Montague drew aside the curtains, just enough to let in a little of the light, and sat down at the pianoforte. Mindlessly, he fingered the notes from a sonata by Haydn. He was halfway through the piece when he felt a presence. Turning around, he found Miss Daliyah, dressed and groomed, standing at the threshold.

"Pray, do not let me interrupt you, my lord," she said. "You play beautifully. Will you not continue?"

"If you will stand by the pianoforte and not skulk behind my back," he replied.

She obliged and moved toward the instrument. He finished the rest of the sonata while she stood listening, at times closing her eyes as if to absorb the music through her body.

"You can vary the volume from loud to soft through this instrument," she noted when he was done.

"Hence its name, the pianoforte. The strings are struck rather than plucked as is done with the harpsichord," he explained.

"Though the harpsichord is a beautiful instrument, I like this one better. You are quite skilled with it."

"I am average at best."

"I cannot imagine better."

"Merely because you have not heard enough people play."

"That may be true, but it does not diminish

the joy I derive from hearing you play. Was it hard to learn?"

He tried to think back on his time as a boy with his music instructor. Unlike Montague's father, the man had been kind to him. Perhaps that was why Montague tolerated the music lessons.

"You may determine for yourself," he said. "Come. Sit."

He shifted to make room for her upon the piano bench.

"But I have chores, and if you wish for breakfast—"

"Your chores can wait."

Without further protest, she sat down beside him. He positioned her hand upon the keys with her thumb at middle C.

"Keep your fingers curled," he told her, rounding his hand over hers.

With his thumb, he pressed down upon her own twice. He did the same with her pinkie finger. He moved the pinkie over the A key and struck it twice before returning it back to the G key for two counts.

"I know this tune!" she exclaimed.

He continued through all her fingers down the scale to her thumb, before going back to the pinkie. Each finger struck its key twice as they descended from high to low. They repeated this before echoing the first progression.

"There," he declared. "You have just played *Ah! vous dirai-je, maman.*"

Her eyes sparkled. Her delight washed over him like a large wave, surprising him with how lovely she looked.

"Thank you, my lord!" she said.

His gaze dropped to her smile. He marveled at the evenness of her teeth and even the plumpness of her lips. What would it feel like to kiss her?

He decided to find out.

Cupping the back of her head, he lowered his own, slowly enough to give her the chance to object. When she did not, he smothered her mouth with his.

Her mouth was every bit as delicious as the rest of her. He took hungry mouthfuls of her. She had tensed at first, but she did not fight him. Heat flamed through him as he delved deeper into her orifice, tasting her from various angles, their warm, uneven breaths mingling as he feasted upon her.

"Did you not have enough of her last night?"

At the sound of Addison's voice, Montague

silently cursed. Miss Daliyah rose from the bench.

"Do you prefer breakfast now or should I feed the animals first?" she asked.

"I will assist you," Addison replied.

"Are you certain?"

"Yes."

Addison returned his gaze to Montague.

"Would you care for breakfast, my lord?" she asked.

"Perhaps later," he replied, cross that his moment with her had been interrupted.

He watched the two of them part. Addison had a sound question, implying he ought to have been satiated from having taken Miss Daliyah not once but twice last night. The answer, which he had begun to suspect in recent days, had nothing to do with the curse.

He desired Miss Daliyah on his own.

Chapter Thirty Six

Seeing the brightness of her room, Daliyah bolted upright in bed. She had slept late! Throwing back the bedclothes, she dressed as quickly as she could. Exhausted last night, she had allowed Addison to undress her. He exerted himself too much on her behalf while still recovering from his wounds. He had likely made breakfast already.

She hurried downstairs. As she reached the foyer, she heard Lord Blackbourne call out her name. She waited till he appeared and expected a scolding for rising so late.

"Forgive me, I had not intended to sleep so late," she said as he took her by the elbow and led her to the dining hall, where a full breakfast with toast, cheese, and fruits awaited.

He pulled out the chair at the head of the table. "Sit, Daliyah."

Bewildered, she raised her brows.

"You are a poor servant to disregard my orders," he said in a stern voice.

At that, she took a seat. She had never sat at the head of the table before.

Addison entered and set a cup down before her. "Chocolate."

Her mouth dropped. Was this all for her?

"You have worked tirelessly and endured much in your time here," said Lord Blackbourne. "And I suspect you had no days off while traveling with Miss Cameron. You are deserving of a respite."

"Today," Addison added, "you are not to lift a finger."

"Not lift a finger?" she echoed. "But how will the chores be done? I could not leave you to finish them all yourself when you have not your full strength."

"Montague intends to assist me."

"Perhaps we can wait till you are better?"

"Addison and I are firm in our decision."

"I have no choice in the matter then?" she asked.

Addison frowned. Lord Blackbourne's jaw

tightened. She regretted her question. Of course a servant in her position had no choice.

"You may choose how you wish to spend your time," Lord Blackbourne said, "provided it involves no work."

"Indeed," Addison seconded. "You may choose to read, pick flowers, embroider. Perhaps you would like a picnic?"

"That sounds lovely," she said.

He smiled. "Then it shall be so. Now drink before the chocolate turns cold."

She picked up the mug and took a sip. Her eyes grew large. What a rich and delicious indulgence was this!

"What of your breakfast?" she asked.

"I have partaken already," Addison answered.

With the two men watching, she hesitated.

"Let us have some coffee or tea while Daliyah enjoys her breakfast," suggested Lord Blackbourne.

Addison went to the sideboard where coffee and tea had already been set up. He poured two cups of coffee for himself and his brother.

"I can taste this coffee," Lord Blackbourne commented after a sip. "The flavor is wanting, but it could be worse."

Addison stared at his brother. "It does not repulse you?"

"It does not," Lord Blackbourne confirmed. He looked over at her. "I see you like the chocolate."

She blushed, realizing she had finished it already.

"I can prepare another," Addison offered.

"No, please," she protested. "This is all more than one person can eat."

"What do you wish to do after breakfast?"

"I could walk the horses?"

"No work."

"But I enjoy walking the horses."

"Very well. And after that?"

She could think of nothing. Finally, she said, "I could pick more bormint."

Addison shook his head.

"You like it when I play the pianoforte," Lord Blackbourne said. "Would you like me to play again?"

"Yes," she replied cheerfully.

After breakfast, she walked the horses with Addison. Lord Blackbourne was ready at the pianoforte when they returned. While his lordship played a rondo, Addison took her hands and whirled her about in dance. She had not danced since her days in Barbados and had forgotten how much she enjoyed it.

They went on a picnic in the early afternoon. After partaking of the food Addison had prepared, she listened to their childhood stories of mischief. She and Addison then strolled along the pond while Lord Blackbourne napped beneath a tree.

She had time to herself before supper while the men worked. After supper, they played several hands of *vingt-et-un*. When it came time for bed, she was sad for the day to come to an end. For the first time, she found Castle Blackbourne neither dark nor forbidding.

Addison had started a fire in the hearth of her chambers and even heated her bed with the warming pans. As she slid into her bed, she marveled at her circumstances. She had spent the day as a lady, in the clothes of a noblewoman, dining at the table of a nobleman, and was now abed in chambers reserved for the gentry.

But more than the trappings of luxury, she was grateful that someone cared for her wellbeing. It was odd that it should come from two men who had wronged her in so many ways, but she preferred to think there was hope for them. She felt convinced of Addison's repentance and sincerity. She could not say the same for Lord Blackbourne. Yet.

He was different than the day she had met him, but could he truly keep his dark side at bay? She recalled their kiss at the pianoforte. Unlike Addison's tender kisses, his lordship's was ravenous. Beneath it, she detected a yearning. For affection, perhaps. There was more to Lord Blackbourne than his curse.

She remembered how he had seen to her euphoria before his own the other night. She had never thought to feel such potent desire and would have taken both men at once if she could. Simply recalling the intensity of her arousal warmed her body.

Her hand slid between her thighs, and she rubbed herself. She remembered the moments of ecstasy she'd had with both men and wondered if she should be concerned that the memories seemed untainted by the brew of desire from Lord Blackbourne's fangs. Pressing the fabric of her chemise against the nub of pleasure between her folds, she stroked the tension to where she wanted not to stop.

But she did when she heard a knock at the door.

"Come in," she said.

It was Addison. He rubbed the back of his neck before saying, "Montague...I think he wishes, tonight—"

"I know."

He approached the bed and sat down. "Is there anything you wish to be done? I am no less committed to serving *your* wishes than before. If you would rather not submit to his desires, I could—"

Grabbing him, she crushed her lips to his. He responded immediately by pulling her closer into his arms. She took several mouthfuls of him before entangling her tongue with his. They spent several minutes exploring the depths of their mouths, till Addison kissed his way down to her neck, passing his tongue over the scars left by Lord Blackbourne's fangs. He pulled her chemise down and kissed her bared shoulders and then her breasts.

She lay back and entwined her fingers into his hair as he took a nipple into his mouth. Each lick, each tug made the area between her legs throb.

He kissed his way down her body, pulled her chemise up past her hips, and settled between her thighs. He combed his fingers through the hair at her mound, kissed the inside of her thigh, and spread her folds with his fingers to reveal the rosebud between.

His tongue met it, making her gasp. Languidly, he licked her, stretching the tension through her body. She gasped more loudly when he flicked his tongue rapidly against her. The need coiled in her belly, concentrating where his tongue fondled, intensified. He dipped his tongue into her wetness and spread the moisture upon her swelling bud of pleasure. She shuddered.

His hunger seemed to flare with hers, and he assaulted her with mouth and tongue with increasing earnestness. She squirmed when he closed his lips about her pleasure nub and sucked. The pressure he had stoked boiled over. With cries and quaking, she spent.

When the wave of euphoria had receded, Addison climbed over her.

"If you could only know how divinely you taste," he murmured before smothering her mouth with his.

She *could* taste herself upon his lips. Her body arched to meet more of his. Though she had just spent, the emptiness in her cunnie ached to be filled.

Mr. Brooke sat back, unbuttoned his fall, and pulled out his spear of arousal. He stroked himself while she came up to her knees and wrapped her mouth about his stiff member. He groaned, then grunted as she eagerly sucked upon his shaft. His hand went to the back of her head, pressing her down to take more of him. As if starved, she consumed as much of him as she could, as fast as she could. When he urged her too far down his length, she gagged. He released her to allow her to cough and catch her breath.

Sitting back against the pillows, he turned her away from him and settled her over his lap. She straddled him, delighted that her cunnie would soon be filled. He angled his member at her slit and, with a hand upon her hip, guided her down.

Her cunnie fluttered and caressed the hardness inside her. He pulled her back against his chest, then reached between her legs to find the nub once more. Pleasure flooded her body. The sweetness of his fingers plying her flesh and the throbbing of his member filling her set her on a new plane of bliss. Closing her eyes, she savored the sensations and tried not to spend too soon.

Her eyes fluttered open when Addison moved

his hips, and she saw Lord Blackbourne standing at the threshold.

Chapter Thirty Seven

Ardor raged inside Montague as he beheld Miss Daliyah half-sitting, half-laying against his brother, her chemise falling off a shoulder to reveal a breast, her legs splayed with Addison's hand between her thighs. He watched as Addison continued to fondle her, his gaze and demeanor laying claim to her.

But it would not be so for long.

Miss Daliyah moaned and writhed atop Addison, her shapely legs, her dark areolas, her supple lips a siren's call to his desire. Approaching the bed, he began to shed his garments one by one. She kept her gaze upon him, perhaps wary of what he might do, but she did not balk. His appearance had not sent her scrambling to hide beneath the bedclothes, as he had half expected.

Addison raised his hips, and with her chemise bunched at her waist, Montague could see Addison's cock buried in her. His fingers quickened at her crotch, making her squirm.

Naked, Montague climbed onto the bed. His cock protruded from his body, long and hard. Partially distracted by Addison's ministrations, she made no protest when Montague knelt before them, but she watched him carefully as he pushed her thighs up and back, further exposing her cunnie. He spread the mettle glistening from his tip over his shaft, then pointed his cock at her.

Could she take two at a time?

As if she heard his query, her eyes widened. He wondered if he should sink his fangs into her to flood her with desire, but he was curious if she would allow this congress of her own volition. He pressed the head of his cock against her flesh.

"Here now—" Addison objected.

Montague gave him a silencing glare, though he saw his brother, too, was curious. Miss Daliyah released a quivering breath as he pushed into her. She groaned, then gasped when he had successfully buried the crown of his cock inside her.

His head swam with how tight she was. It was beyond anything he had ever felt before.

Addison cursed, but he had to feel the same. Miss Daliyah panted. Her brow furrowed intensely. She lay her head back and attempted to relax.

"I know not that she can accommodate—" Addison said.

"She can," Montague said. "And she will."

Slowly, he sank himself farther. She gave a shaky whimper.

"Fondle her," Montague ordered Addison, who had stopped his ministrations upon Montague's entry.

Addison resumed, his fingers plying her clitoris till her lashes fluttered and she moaned in pleasure. Montague continued his progress till more than half his cock was sheathed inside her. Closing his eyes, he relished the tight embrace of her cunnie. Beneath his cock, his brother's hardened arousal throbbed.

Gradually, Montague withdrew, his cock sliding against Addison's. Miss Daliyah murmured beneath her breath.

"Damn me!" Addison murmured.

Changing course, Montague pressed forward, feeling near delirious with the pressure encasing him. It took much effort to restrain himself from pounding into such glory, but from her quivers and grunts, he gathered Miss Daliyah had never had her cunnie stretched in this manner. She held up admirably, her body continuing to generate moisture, coating his path.

Several minutes passed by before she seemed more at ease with being speared by two cocks. He could feel her cunnie flexing about them, grasping or resisting he could not tell, but it felt marvelous either way.

"I am near to spending," Addison said.

Montague paused. He held her gaze. "Spend for us first, my dear."

Addison quickened his fingers against her engorged rosebud. Montague grasped her breast and tugged at her nipple. Leaning over her, he cupped her chin and covered her lips with his. He felt her heavy breaths, felt her cunnie clench upon him. He delved his tongue into her mouth.

She came undone, her cries muffled by his mouth. Her body trembled and bucked and might have come off Addison if Montague had not held her down. He shoved his cock deeper. Addison spent next, flooding her with liquid heat.

The sensations overwhelmed him, and

Montague joined in their pinnacle of ecstasy.

They lay panting, their bodies joined, pulsing, throbbing, perspiring, and bathed in euphoria. Montague withdrew after his cock had softened.

"My God," Miss Daliyah murmured in relief.

"That was..." Addison began, but had not the words to complete his sentence.

"Agreed," Montague said as he sat back.

Addison kept Miss Daliyah in his arms. She lay against him with her eyes closed. Montague could not help a stab of jealousy.

Leaving the two, he collected his clothes and returned to his own chambers, where he reflected on the fact that Miss Daliyah had not needed his fangs. Had she resigned herself to her fate or did she now desire him?

Perhaps it was Addison she wished to please, Addison for whom she spent...but it was promising that she had allowed Montague into her.

Theirs was an odd arrangement, to be sure, but the curse had torn asunder any normalcy in his life. Though, after years of searching and despairing, he finally had hope. Now all he had to do was refrain from falling in love with her, but he worried that he had already begun to do so.

For now, he would do better to dwell on his good fortune and the promise of a better future... for he had found his Beauty.

Printed in Great Britain
by Amazon

41362729R00175